"What beck'ning ghost along
Invites my step and points

With Best Wishes

*[signature]*

14. ix. 99.

"Then suddenly, through the haze of smoke and steam, there he was. A slight, dark haired lad ... standing motionless, his pale face pressed against the misted glass of the carriage window.

For some unaccountable reason, I was shivering. But why should the mere sight of a boy who I hadn't seen before ... have such an effect upon me?"

And why indeed?

Shropshire, December 1918. The War to End all Wars is finally over. Live is slowly returning to normal. But for Stephen Harris, a young solicitor with the old established Hereford firm of Evans, Chapman and Jenkins, the next few days will be anything but normal.

Eagerly looking forward to spending the last week end before Christmas walking the hills of south Shropshire, blissfully unaware of what awaits him, he takes the early morning train northwards, to Ludlow.

To begin with there is nothing out of the ordinary. Everything seems quite normal. Then gradually a disturbing series of incidents take place, increasingly incapable of rational explanation, and which seem somehow linked to lonely Marsh Leys Hall, and the appearance of a mysterious dark haired boy.

Years later, the painful memory of what took place then is vividly rekindled for Stephen by the recurrence of an old nightmare. But why should it have returned to haunt him now?

# Whistle And I'll Be There

A Ghost Story of Shropshire and the Marches

by

JONATHAN MOOR

HORSESHOE PUBLICATIONS . WARRINGTON . CHESHIRE

© 1997 Jonathan Moor

ALL RIGHTS RESERVED

No part of this book may be reproduced in any form by photocopying or by any electronic or mechanical means including information storage or retrieval systems without prior permission in writing from both the copyright owner and the publisher of this book.

ISBN 1 899310.04.5

British Library Cataloguing in Publication Data
A catalogue record for this book is available from The British Library

First published 1997 by
HORSESHOE PUBLICATIONS
Box 37, Kingsley, Warrington,
Cheshire WA6 8DR

Book cover designed
by Philip Jackson of Cheshire

Printed and bound in Great Britain by
Redwood Books Ltd
Trowbridge, Wilts

"But if you come to a road where danger
Or guilt or anguish or shame's to share,
Be good to the lad that loves you true
And the soul that was born to die for you,
And whistle and I'll be there"

A.E. Housman

*For My Parents*

# All Hallows Eve

Midnight. All Hallows Eve. The witching hour, a peculiar choice of time you will think, no doubt, to be taking a nocturnal stroll round the garden, but that is precisely what I was doing.

I hadn't been able to sleep. That in itself wasn't unusual, but tonight was different. Once again, for the third time in as many weeks, I'd had the same dream. The one I'd experienced all those years ago, and which until these past few weeks, I thought I'd finally exorcised from the innermost recesses of my mind.

For sometime I lay awake in the darkness, desperately trying to fathom out why it should have returned to haunt me now. Downstairs the clock in the hall struck eleven, and then a while later I heard it chime the half hour.

I turned over and tried to go back to sleep. But sleep wouldn't come. In an odd sort of a way, I suppose I was thankful for that. Ever present at the back of my mind was the gnawing fear that if I slept, the dream would start all over again.

Eventually I could stand it no longer. Not wishing to disturb Claire, I dressed quietly, came downstairs, let myself out of the silent, sleeping house, and made my way down here to the white painted summer house at the bottom of the garden on the banks of the Wensum.

Of all the seasons, I think autumn is still the one I love best - the falling leaves, its glowing colours, the mists, its mellow fruitfulness, the smell of bonfires, and leaf mould carpeting the ground underfoot.

So, inhaling the damp autumn night air with undisguised pleasure, I made my way across the darkened lawns, past the lily pond, over towards the sundial which stood at the far end of the stone flagged path.

I carried on down the flight of steps leading to the lower terrace and the sunken rose garden, which Claire had laid out soon after our arrival here in Norwich.

Threading my way through the rhododendrons, the twigs crackling under my feet, I mused briefly on the more fanciful tales told of goblins and witches, ghosts and spirits, said to walk the earth this night. The one night of the year when the dead hold court and the living, if they are wise, stay safe and snug behind bolted doors and shuttered windows.

Since my childhood in Shropshire, I'd always been interested in folklore and had regarded such tales as no more than that, harmless stories told by parents to wide eyed children gathered round the fireside on a winter's night. Of no more

*Whistle . . .*

consequence than the games played by young and old alike with nuts and apples to celebrate the old New Year's Eve, when everything is touched with strangeness.

Indeed, there can be few parts of the kingdom where there are more varied customs connected with Hallowe'en than Shropshire and the Welsh Marches. As a boy I well recall going guising round the streets of Market Drayton in the company of my cousins Robert and Samuel, all three of us with blackened faces, dressed in the weirdest of clothes, and asking passers-by for pennies, apples, oranges and nuts.

And when we got home, once we'd been thoroughly washed and scrubbed in the nursery upstairs, sneaking back downstairs to the warm kitchen, where we cajoled and pleaded with our cook Mrs Chetwynd into letting us bob for apples in a wooden pail, filled almost to the brim with cold water, set in the middle of the long kitchen table, and getting thoroughly soaked in the process. We got a leathering afterwards, but it was worth it!

Childhood apart, I'd spent the first few years of my working life in the same area, first as an articled clerk with a firm of solicitors in Market Drayton in the north east part of the county, and latterly as a solicitor in my own right in private practice with Evans, Chapman and Jenkins in Hereford, prior to obtaining a position with Broome, Challoner and Deakin here in Norwich.

Sitting here alone in the darkness, musing on the past, it was to Hereford that my thoughts returned now, prompted in part I suppose by the scene before me. The mist slowly rising from off the river, and beyond it, in the distance, the outline of the cathedral and the spires of the city churches showing black against the night sky. All serving to remind me of another night, thankfully long since past.

Yet the memory of it lingers. Is with me still, and, I suppose, always will be. For there are throughout a man's life, I truly believe, experiences which remain with him always, even unto the very hour of his death.

We'd moved to Norwich shortly after our marriage and bought Blakeney Lodge in the spring of the following year. The contrast between the countryside of East Anglia and the scenery of my native Shropshire could not have been more pronounced. I must confess, the flat low lying Fens, the watery expanse of the Broads with their deep reed fringed, wild bird-haunted creeks, and the Norfolk coastline with its seemingly limitless vistas of sand, sea and sky, took some getting used to.

I remember reading, I forget where now, of a children's nanny, who when the family she worked for moved from Norfolk to the Lake District, to Grasmere I

*. . . and I'll be there*

think, complained she felt unable to breathe and that the mountains spoiled the view! I can sympathise with how she must have felt.

Since we moved over to Norfolk, I have never once been back to the county of my birth, nor even to that part of England. Like Housman, who wrote so longingly of the county in that wonderful prose poem of his *'A Shropshire Lad'*, I can never go back there again. Of that I am certain.

And yet, strange as it may seem, despite my love of Shropshire and the Welsh Marches, I have no desire to do so. Indeed, I count myself fortunate that I no longer have any relations living in that part of the country, and that our remaining friends in the county have long ceased asking us to visit them.

To begin with, I mean, it was easy to make excuses. I was able to plead pressure of work, that the children were too young to make the journey, Claire was indisposed, in fact a whole host of reasons, none of which I am sure were believed for a moment.

Even when Simon and Andrew eventually went away to school in Hereford, it was Claire, not I, who went with them on the train, at least until they were old enough to make the journey unaccompanied. Although Claire thought me unduly sensitive at the time, I would have vastly preferred it if the boys had gone somewhere else, rather than the Cathedral School in Hereford.

Curious that. After all Claire alone knows the real reason behind my refusal to return to Shropshire. Also, since I told her, I have never spoken of it to anyone, save one other person, and she is now no longer among the living.

For myself the past is still too close. Even after all these years. Disturbingly so. For why else should the same dream have returned to haunt me now? Bringing in its wake echoes of something best left forgotten. Left undisturbed. Which, for my own peace of mind, and also for the sake of those I love, must stay buried. Otherwise the memory of that which I have tried to forget and put behind me would stir again, and with it too, blind unreasoning panic. The painful memory of which I had hoped would dim and fade with the passage of time.

With the passing years, I must concede that this has indeed come to pass. At least to some extent. And memory - thank God - is indeed merciful. But even now I have to but to close my eyes and I can recall every detail of that most singular experience as if it had happened yesterday, instead of nearly half a century ago.

I think Claire suspects that something is amiss. The other day, after dinner, while we were waiting for James to bring in the coffee, I caught her looking at me in such a wistful fashion, but she had the good sense to refrain from asking if anything was troubling me, either then or later, and the moment passed. For once

*Whistle . . .*

I was grateful that we had guests, even if they did include the garrulous Major Wilson and his odious little wife, Margaret.

After our arrival in Norwich, to begin with we rented a small house just off Elm Hill, not far from the cathedral, right in the heart of the city, while we looked round for a property which would be suitable both for entertaining and as a family home, which the house in Elm Hill, with its cramped accommodation and tiny walled garden, patently was not.

As is the way with such things, we came across Blakeney Lodge, quite by chance, whilst out for a leisurely drive one Sunday afternoon. The then owners Colonel and Mrs Jefferson were in much the same position as we are today. Their children had grown up and left home, and they were finding the upkeep of a large house and extensive grounds increasingly beyond them.

We made an appointment with the agents to view the property and fell in love with it immediately. We had nowhere to sell, and accordingly we were able to come to an amicable arrangement regarding the purchase price, which was acceptable to both parties.

I even did most of the conveyancing myself, the first such transaction of that sort which I'd handled since my dealings with Marsh Leys Hall in Shropshire.

One approaches Blakeney Lodge by way of a long sweeping drive, flanked on either side by Horse Chestnuts. Sadly, last November, we lost three of the trees in a gale. The house itself isn't particularly old. It was built round the turn of the century, for one of the directors of the old Great Eastern Railway company. Mock Tudor in style, with stone mullioned windows and delightfully ornate twisted brick chimney stacks.

I rather like the stone flagged entrance hall with its elaborate plaster ceiling and oak wood panelling. It is also the only room in the entire house still lit by oil lamps. I know Claire considers it to be dark and gloomy, but short of installing electric light and ripping out the panelling, which is something I would never countenance, the hall is the one room of the house which so far has defied Claire's improving hand.

Although the property was in a reasonable state of repair when we moved in, shortly thereafter Claire embarked upon a systematic redecoration of the entire house, excepting the hall of course, together with various improvements to the grounds.

The principal rooms of the house, the dining room, the library and the drawing room all open off the hall and lie on the south side, with sweeping views across the river to the city beyond. From the drawing room, you can step outside directly onto the upper terrace, where, during the summer, Claire and I often sit to have supper.

One of the most attractive features of both the house and grounds are the terraced gardens, descending to the banks of the Wensum. The sunken rose garden below the lower terrace was the first of many alterations Claire made to the outside of the house. The stone urns placed along the balustrade of the upper terrace, together with the summerhouse, where I'm sitting now, came later.

It was just as well that Claire's alterations to the house and gardens were sympathetic and largely unobtrusive, as for several years after we'd purchased the property, the Jeffersons came back to visit us whenever they were in Norwich. But after Colonel Jefferson became too ill to travel, we continued visiting them in their new home in Thetford, eventually we became firm friends.

I suspect one of the reasons why we struck up such a warm friendship was that we retained the services of several of their domestic staff, including both their housekeeper - the redoubtable Mrs Whitfield, and the head gardener, Fellows.

Eventually, the Jeffersons came to assume the role of supernumerary grandparents to both our boys Simon and Andrew. Both Colonel Jefferson and his wife died some years ago now, and I suspect our boys miss them as much as we do.

While Simon and Andrew were growing up, both of them spent many pleasant hours messing about on the Wensum, learning first to swim and then to row. Simon in particular took to both like the proverbial duck to water, as a result of which I had the old boat-house down on the river thoroughly renovated.

Simon's early promise was fully realised when he was chosen to row for the county of Norfolk, despite him being a boarder at the Cathedral School in Hereford. After school, and several false starts, Simon opted eventually for a career in the Colonial Service. He's now a District Commissioner out in Nyasaland, having met his wife Helen in Kenya while on a posting to Nairobi, where she was nursing in the General Hospital.

Simon and Helen decided to leave both their children, Timothy (he prefers to be called Tim) and young David here with us in England, at least until both the boys are of an age to be sent away to boarding school. For the time being they go to the King Edward VI School here in Norwich. It's an arrangement which suits us all very well, and I'm sure Claire would be the first to agree this rambling great house would seem rather empty without Tim and David. However, when they've finished school in Norwich, I think it will then be time for Claire and myself to look for somewhere smaller. After all neither of us are getting any younger.

*Whistle . . .*

Andrew, on the other hand, was the more academic of our two boys. He went up to Cambridge, to St. John's College, where he read History and Classics, gaining a double first. I say that with no trace of conceit. With the amount of work he put in, it was no more than he deserved.

Eventually he went out to Canada, having secured a lectureship in history at the McGill University in Montreal. To begin with he found lodgings through the kindness of a very dear friend of mine who, having inherited some property in Quebec, had recently returned to Canada after nearly a lifetime spent in England. The following year, Andrew met his future wife Mary, while on holiday, or should I say vacation, in the Rockies, not far from Lake Louise.

They've three children now, the twins Richard and William, Richard incidentally takes after his uncle Simon in his love of sports, and Emily - the baby of the family. She's six now and looks very like Claire did at the same age. They came back to England several years ago, and settled in the Cotswolds, at Burford, not far from Oxford, where Andrew had obtained a senior lectureship, this time in Medieval Studies.

Earlier this afternoon I'd come down to the scullery in search of Mrs Holt, successor to the redoubtable Mrs Whitfield, to find both her and Claire seated at the kitchen table, entering with gusto into the festive spirit of the occasion, busily engaged scooping out a turnip for a Hallowe'en lantern for our youngest grandson David, all of eight years old, shortly to be nine, and now fast asleep upstairs in the night nursery, no doubt dreaming of his forthcoming birthday and the party to celebrate it, to be held here at the house a week on Sunday.

I hope earnestly for young David, as I do for all the rest of our grandchildren, Timothy, William, Richard and little Emily, that such ghostly tales remain just that and no more. They are harmless, as far as they go.

The reality is far more prosaic, and because of that far more chilling and far more terrifying than anything you could possibly imagine, unless you have experienced it for yourself.

As I have.

*. . . and I'll be there*

# A Winter's Afternoon

The day I first saw the manor house, winter dusk was fast falling across the frozen Shropshire countryside. The woods and fields lay silent under a thick white shroud of freshly fallen snow, which glistened with an intensity that all but blinded the eye.

I'd spent most of that Saturday afternoon, the last before Christmas, walking the hills near Ludlow. At that time, I could think of few pleasanter ways of working off the excesses of the festive season than a brisk afternoon's walk in the hills of south Shropshire.

Although I'd been brought up in a town, albeit a market town at that, and in the flatter north eastern part of the county, I loved the peace and solitude of the south-western hills, particularly in winter. There you could walk for miles, perhaps you still can, and not see sight nor sign of human habitation, let alone another human being.

Indeed, that particular Saturday I found the prospect of a brisk walk in the hills even more exhilarating than usual, having had to spend the previous week up in town on business. I must confess, apart from visits to the theatre or museums, I do not like London.

Claire, my fiancée, had declined to come with me. She had, she told me rather solemnly I thought, decided to stay put in Hereford. In her view, the comforts of a warm fire and a good book were infinitely preferable to the dubious pleasures to be got from tramping the snow bound hills of Shropshire in deep mid winter.

I thought I caught a twinkle of mischief in her eyes as she spoke. But that apart, I must have looked extremely crestfallen. I've never been very good at concealing my feelings. Claire, always the one for practical jokes, could contain herself no longer and burst out laughing.

She would, she said, have loved to come with me, as well I knew. But being an only child, and this, the last Christmas before we were married, she felt she should spend most of it with her parents.

In any event, had I forgotten the Christmas Eve concert she and her fellow members of the Hereford Choral Society were giving in All Saints' Church? There was a final rehearsal at the church scheduled for Saturday afternoon, and she couldn't possibly miss it.

"Go off and enjoy yourself," she said, laughingly, and so I did.

*Whistle . . .*

Had I any inkling of what lay ahead, then I should not have gone. But then, how could I, or indeed anyone else for that matter, have known, have even guessed at, what I know now?

I made what few preparations I needed to make with the alacrity of a boy down from boarding school for the Christmas holidays. I decided it would make more sense if I spent the Saturday night in Ludlow. Claire raised no objection, so I wired ahead and booked myself a room in The Bell Inn at Ludford, just across the River Teme from Ludlow.

That Saturday morning I caught the early train north from Hereford. Claire saw me off from Barrs Court station. Surprisingly, the train kept reasonably well to time, arriving in Ludlow shortly after ten o'clock.

I was in high spirits and impatient to be off. Westwards, the snow clad hills beckoned. Shouldering my rucksack, I strode briskly down the road leading from the station, and made my way out of town by way of the little stone bridge spanning the River Corve, which flows into the Teme just above Ludlow. A mile or so further on, and I found the stile I was seeking. Clambering over it, dislodging a shower of snow in the process, I left the road behind me and set off across the fields, towards the Teme. As I did so, the faintest of breezes stirred the frost hung boughs of the trees, bringing down a gentle dusting of snow. There had been a hard frost during the night so, for the time being at least, animals and birds alike left no trace of their passage across the empty frozen countryside.

I walked on. Behind me the sun crept higher and higher into the sky, which gradually melted from the orange of sunrise into a deep and brilliant shade of blue, more in keeping with a day in late July, than one in deep December. Glorious weather in fact, for walking in the hills.

The air was bright and clear. Indeed it remained that way for most of the day. It was only now, on my way back to Ludlow, as the sun sank lower behind the western hills and the dusk drew down, that the light began to fade from the sky. By my own reckoning I must have walked well over twenty miles that day. Thankfully the snow had kept off, but judging by the heavy clouds drifting in from the east, there would be more before nightfall.

I crunched down the snow covered track, back towards the stream. I'd crossed it during the morning, higher up, near its source above Downton. Far above me a solitary sparrowhawk circled in the frost hung air, its plaintive "kek-kek-kek" echoing across the frozen landscape.

Cautiously I edged over the wooden two plank bridge. The handrail was stiff with rime, the surface of the bridge slippery with frost, sparkling in the last rays

*. . . and I'll be there*

of the setting sun. Beneath me, the sibilant slate-grey waters of the fast flowing stream, swollen by several weeks of heavy rain, tumbled their way downhill towards the Teme. At the time I remember thinking if it turned much colder, the stream would probably freeze over.

Once on the other side, the ground began to rise sharply upwards, towards the last ridge of high ground, below which, presently lost to sight, lay the border town of Ludlow.

Pressing onwards, I began clambering up the bank. Ahead of me the snow lay thick and undisturbed, save for what looked suspiciously like the tracks of a polecat, and those of numerous small birds. The dark branches of the trees hung motionless in the still air, laden down with their heavy burden of snow.

It was just as I reached the top of the ridge that I caught sight of the manor house for the first time. In fact, if I hadn't been following the soaring flight of the sparrowhawk, I might not even have seen it at all.

The house lay below me, away to my right, all but hidden from sight by the lie of the land, sheltered from the prevailing wind by the high ground to the north and by a dense area of woodland stretching away to the south and west.

Away to the east lay Ludlow. In the distance I could just make out the snow covered ruins of the castle, the tall tower of St Laurence's Church and the huddle of houses clustered round them. I wasn't expected at the inn until about six, so being somewhat curious, if for no other reason, I turned and slithered my way back down to the foot of the bank, to where the house lay nestling in the batch.

From a distance it looked no different to any other house of a similar date and style such as Plaish Hall, or Wilderhope Manor over in the Corvedale, both of which I knew well, having bicycled out to them the previous summer with Claire, while we were staying with her aunt at Rushbury, not far from the ancient market town of Much Wenlock with its ruined priory and half timbered Guildhall.

As I drew closer, it became clear that the house was empty. No-one lived here. At least not any more. I think my overwhelming impression was one of loneliness, tinged with grief and sadness, and a sense of loss and bereavement. Yet there had been a time, not long since, when the house glowed with lamplight and warmth. When its now forsaken rooms rang with the merry sound of a child's laughter. How I knew that I couldn't say. But know it I most emphatically did.

Also there was something else. Even now I find it difficult to convey in words what I felt on seeing the house for the very first time. An aura of stillness enfolded the entire building, right down to the very stones of its foundations, from whence a profound silence seemed to well up, like water from a spring. It was almost as

9

*Whistle . . .*

if the house was waiting for something, or perhaps someone.

Bounded by a low stone wall what must once have been a terraced garden climbed gently upwards towards the house, which from where I was standing, looked as though it might once have been larger.

To my right stood the stable block, surmounted by a small wooden cupola, beneath which was a clock, its face badly weathered, the numerals all but effaced. Not surprisingly the hands stood still - stopped at a quarter past three. Behind the stable block were several other outbuildings, mostly ruinous, including what looked like the remains of a small dovecote.

Behind me, stretched what was once a wide drive, now not much more than an overgrown track, which wound away between the overhanging trees.

In front of me there had once been a pair of gates. But one of the pillars had long since collapsed. Its stones lay tumbled at my feet. Looking somewhat forlorn a single rusty iron gate still hung from the remaining pillar, which was topped rather improbably by a large carved stone pineapple.

I pushed open the gate as far as I dared, dislodging a shower of snow, then climbed a short flight of steps, and set off across the garden towards the house. In fact at times, so heavy were the drifts of snow, it was difficult to be certain if I was keeping to the path. Not that I suppose it really mattered.

Halfway between the house and the gate, I came upon a circular stone pool, all but buried beneath the snow, the frozen reeds of which protruded stiffly through the ice. Skirting round the pool, I climbed another set of steps, and shortly afterwards found myself standing on a small, stone flagged terrace, before the south front of the house.

The building was, after all, larger than at first I'd thought, in part half timbered, the wood bleached to a pale silver grey by countless years of exposure to the wind and rain. But the greater part of the house was built of the same weathered grey stone as the stable block, with a jettied upper storey, and mullioned windows.

There were two massive brick chimney stacks. The larger of the two, pierced by narrow wind breaks, stood at the rear of the building. It looked to be in a very poor state of repair. The joints gaped open, much of the mortar was missing, and several courses of brickwork had fallen away from the top. The other chimney, built against the gable at the west end of the house, showed similar signs of disrepair. Halfway up it, a small stunted bush had even taken root.

The roof was mostly hidden beneath a heavy covering of snow, but from what I could see, it looked like it was tiled. Here and there, especially near the ridge,

*. . . and I'll be there*

large areas of tiling had fallen away, exposing the roof timbers beneath, which stood out pale and skeletal against the darkening December sky.

The guttering, where it survived, was of cast iron, now rusty with age and neglect. Long pointed icicles hung down from several of the joints. One of the downpipes had broken off several feet above the ground. Just below it stood a wooden water barrel. I lifted the lid. Inside it smelt brackish, the water frozen solid. Round the bottom of the butt patches of ice had formed, glinting briefly in the fading sunlight of the winter's afternoon.

The whole scene brought vividly to my mind part of the opening verse of that well-known carol "In the Bleak Midwinter":

> *Earth stood hard as iron,*
> *Water like a stone.*

The stone window frames were badly decayed, the sills covered with a light powdering of snow and many of the leaded lights were either cracked or broken.

I walked into the porch. In front of me was a heavy door, formed of massive oak planks, studded with iron nails. The bottom of the door was all but lost to sight, hidden beneath a deep bank of snow, driven into the porch by the force of the wind.

Grasping hold of the latch I pressed firmly down on it, at the same time pushing hard against the door with my shoulder. It refused to open. I tried again, and not surprisingly, met with the same result. The door remained firmly closed. Presumably locked and barred from within, as I could see no sign of a keyhole from without.

Wading through the snowdrifts I made my way round the outside of the building, stopping briefly to rub the glass of one of the downstairs windows with my glove.

I peered in. The room was very dark, but through the film of cobwebs and grime covering the inside of the window, I made out a heavily beamed ceiling, and beneath it, a cracked quarry tile floor. In the far corner stood an old cast iron range. Large areas of plaster had fallen away from the walls, littering the floor, and what remained of the wallpaper hung in mildewed shreds. Everything spoke of damp and decay.

At the back of the room a door stood tantalisingly ajar, revealing the foot of a narrow back staircase, no doubt leading to what must once have been the servants' quarters. There was another door to the right of the first. It too stood open. Through it I caught sight of some stone steps, leading downwards. Presumably to a cellar. Despite the fact that I was warmly dressed for walking in the hills, suddenly I found myself shivering.

By now a chill wind had begun to blow, tossing the branches of the trees on

*Whistle . . .*

the bank high above my head back and forth, whipping up fine particles of snow from off the frozen landscape, turning them into icy sprays, which stung my cheeks and seemed capable of penetrating through the several layers of my clothing.

I walked on, round to the rear of the building. Here the snow was much deeper, driven into thick drifts by the force of the wind, which had all but blocked the narrow gully, that lay between the manor house and the steeply rising hillside behind it.

I stood by the back door and stamped my feet hard on the frozen ground to improve the circulation. As I did so, I noticed the imprint of a pair of boy's boots, leading away from the door, across the snow, towards the derelict stable block and the ruinous outbuildings behind it.

Above my head the first few flakes of a fresh fall of snow began to drift down languidly out of the sky. I shivered and looked up. The wind was from the east. Above me the sky was all but lost to sight, hidden beneath a dense mass of whirling white flakes, feathering the air. Behind me both my own footprints, and those of the boy, were rapidly disappearing, hidden beneath the fresh fall of snow. "Time to be off", I thought.

I made my way round to the front of the house, then headed down across the terraced garden, and back towards the gate.

Just by the pool I came upon a further set of footprints, similar, if indeed not identical, to those I'd just seen, interweaving closely with my own. The boy's footprints led on up the steps towards the house. Judging by the amount of freshly fallen snow in each, both sets of prints appeared to have been made at the same time. Which of course was impossible. After all I was on my own. That apart, I hadn't seen anyone else about.

Reaching the gate I pulled it to behind me. Force of habit I suppose, and as I did so, turned to take one last look at the manor house. It was just then, out of the corner of my eye, through the heavy veil of falling snow, that I caught sight of a young dark-haired boy standing near the porch. He looked to be no more than nine or ten, though, at that distance, it was difficult to be sure. Probably a lad from the neighbouring farm. That, at any rate, I thought, solved who'd made the footprints.

I turned away, fumbling with the belt on my jacket, pulling it tighter to keep out the driving snow. But when I looked back, the boy had disappeared.

*. . . and I'll be there*

# Between Sunset and Moonrise

By the time that I reached Ludlow, it was already quite dark. The roofs of the houses and shops, covered by a blanket of snow, stood out stark and white against the inky blackness of the night sky. Most of the buildings were in complete darkness. Here and there the warm glow of lamplight spilled out through an uncurtained window onto the icy pavements of the narrow streets where the snow lay thick and undisturbed. It seemed unlikely anyone would bother clearing it until Monday morning.

Not surprisingly there were few people about, for after all it was bitterly cold. The town lay quiet, seemingly muffled beneath the swirl of softly falling snow. I trudged up Corve Street, past the Feathers Hotel, crunching through the hard packed snow of the Bull Ring, past the Butter Cross, heading for The Bell Inn which lay on the far side of the town, across the Teme, just beyond Ludford Bridge. Above me, snow continued to fall out of the sky, shrouding the ancient buildings of the town still further under a mantle of frosty white.

I walked on down Broad Street, under the Broad Gate, and headed on, still downhill, towards the river and Ludford Bridge. Ahead, slightly to my left, the squat tower of St. Giles's Church stood out against the night sky.

I was about halfway across the bridge, when something made me stop dead in my tracks. I turned round and glanced up the silent, snow-covered street. Nothing, and yet ...

An icy blast of wind whipped up a sudden gust of snow from off the parapet of the bridge. Through the whirling flakes, I caught sight of a young boy, standing motionless under the arch of the Broad Gate at the far end of the street.

Behind me, on the other side of the bridge, the inn sign creaked to and fro on its rusty hinges in the gust of wind. I turned round and glanced up. The name of the inn was all but lost to sight under a thick coating of snow and ice. But when I looked back towards the Broad Gate, the boy had gone, the street was completely deserted.

I crossed over the bridge and carried on up the road. A few moments later, I reached The Bell. Leaving the empty, snow-shrouded street, I ducked down under the low archway and made my way along the cobbled alleyway which led in from the street to the rear of the inn, carefully skirting the ice encrusted doors covering the drop to the cellar.

*Whistle . . .*

Beyond the far end of the passage the courtyard of the inn lay empty and silent. Here the snow was much thicker. But although it was nearly opening time, the inn was in complete darkness.

By the side of the door hung a large brass bell. Rather appropriate I thought, given the name of the inn so I rang it. Several minutes passed. I stood my ground and waited. A short while later I heard footsteps, followed by the sound of bolts being drawn back.

The heavy wooden door swung open on its hinges, revealing a stone flagged passage. Standing in the doorway was a small, stocky man, whom I took to be the landlord. I judged him to be about forty, perhaps a little younger, thick-set and strong, with thinning sandy hair, and a nose which looked as if it had once been broken. He was holding an oil lamp.

"Yes?", he said gruffly.

"I've booked a room for the night."

The man looked at me blankly.

"You're the landlord? I wired ahead."

He scratched his head.

"Arr, yes. Now I be rememberin'. My missus, she dealt with all that. You'd be the young chap ... from 'ereford is it?"

"Yes, Stephen Harris."

"Come in sir. Room's all ready for yer. Number five up the stairs, at the front. 'ere, I'll show yer. No luggage sir?"

"None at all. Apart from this". I indicated the large rucksack on my shoulders.

"Arr, that's right sir, come to think of it, the missus said yer be doin' a spot of walkin', 'ow bin yer day?"

"Fine, thankyou. Although it's started snowing again."

He looked past me into the darkness, seemingly seeking confirmation of the fact.

"Arr, that it has."

He limped ahead of me down the short passage, lit by a single sputtering gas jet, to the foot of a narrow winding staircase, which he informed me led upstairs to the bedrooms above the snug. I waited in near total darkness, whilst the landlord fetched me both the key to my room and a lighted oil lamp.

Outside the night air had been cold and crisp. Here, within the confines of the narrow passage, I was doubly assailed by the smell of cooking, mingled with the reek of cigarette smoke and stale beer. Above my head the gas jet fizzed and sputtered.

*. . . and I'll be there*

The landlord came back a few moments later and handed me my key and the lamp, then gave me directions to my room. As far as supper was concerned, if I'd like to come down to the snug in about half an hour or so?

I climbed up the steep winding staircase, the treads of which creaked at my every step. At the head of the stairs was a small landing, off which, leading in different directions, were several darkened passages. Evidently the gas supply didn't reach upstairs.

I turned to my right, and made my way down the narrow uncarpeted passage, my footsteps echoing noisily on the bare wooden boards. Half way along it, I turned down another short passage, which led to my room at the front of the inn, overlooking the street.

Unlocking the door to my room I let myself in. A bright fire burned in the cast iron grate and a small hod of coal stood ready in the hearth. Setting down the lamp on the round oak table at the foot of the bed, I heaved off my rucksack. Discarding my cap and gloves, I tossed them down on the bed. Then, having hung up my jacket and scarf on the back of the door, I crossed the room, knelt on a chair and looked out of the window.

Condensation trickled down the glass and collected in little pools on the window ledge. The ill-fitting metal casement was stuffed with a damp wad of newspaper to keep out the worst of the draught. I rubbed the glass with the palm of my hand and peered out into the darkness beyond. It seemed to have stopped snowing, at least for the time being. The snow lay thick, sparkling in the moonlight, blanketing the roofs and chimney pots of the houses across the Teme.

I decided to have a wash before going downstairs for supper. A small cracked enamel basin stood in the far corner of the room by the door. I walked over and turned on the tap. Surprisingly I found I had hot water. I poured in cold from the ewer which stood next to the basin on top of the large old-fashioned chest of drawers.

Whilst I was washing, soft footfalls sounded in the passage outside my room. No doubt a benighted traveller stranded by the snow, needing accommodation for the night, and who'd lost his way upstairs in the maze of darkened passages.

Having finished washing, I dressed, placed a fresh shovelful of coal on the fire, turned down the lamp, opened the door and went out into the passage.

As I shut the door behind me, I had the distinct impression that someone had just gone round the corner ahead of me into the other passage leading to the staircase. Nothing unusual in that. Probably another guest. Locking the door, I pocketed the key, and went downstairs to the snug.

*Whistle...*

Except for the landlord, there was no-one else in the room. The stone-flagged floor looked newly scrubbed.

Apart from a solitary oil lamp standing on top of the bar and the flickering gleam cast by two gas jets, the only other light came from the flames of a log fire, roaring away in the massive inglenook fireplace at the far end of the low ceilinged heavily beamed room.

I ordered a tankard of cider. Supper was beef and mushroom pie with vegetables, followed by apple tart and custard. I must confess the very thought of it made my mouth water. I'd lunched on bread and cheese, in the tap room of the Sun Inn at Leintwardine, but I'd had nothing since then, and during the afternoon I'd worked up quite an appetite.

"I'll tell the missus yer be wantin' supper."

The landlord disappeared off into the kitchen. In the ensuing silence, somewhere upstairs, I heard the unmistakeable click of a door latch dropping to and the sound of light footsteps overhead. Probably my mysterious elusive fellow-guest.

For elusive he remained. No-one came downstairs to join me in the snug. I sat by myself on the large oak settle beside the fire, sipped my cider, toasted my feet and stared into the flames. Every so often the logs spat and sizzled. Firelight flickered on the walls of the room, glinted off the polished brasswork and cast shadows across the beamed ceiling.

The landlord came back a few moments later. Supper would be ready directly. He didn't expect much custom that night, if indeed any at all.

"Anyone else staying the night?" I asked.

"No, only yerself sir. Why d'yer ask?"

"Oh, I thought I heard someone in the passage outside my room, I must have been mistaken."

"It's an old house sir, and it makes noises. It'll be the timbers creakin'."

While I waited for my supper, I went and stood at the bar. Both his boys had fought in the War, the eldest Tom with the Yeomanry in Palestine, his youngest lad Jack on the Western Front. He'd been killed near Hautmont, on the Sambre river, shortly before the War had ended.

To begin with, Jack had been merely posted as missing. Then, about a week ago, that had come. That was a buff coloured envelope, standing propped against the wall, on the shelf behind the bar.

The landlord didn't find it surprising the official confirmation had taken so long to arrive. Not with all the chaos and confusion over there in France. But until

*. . . and I'll be there*

it came, his wife had clung to the faint hope that the lad was still alive. But he'd known. Known the boy was dead.

I expressed my condolences. The landlord nodded his thanks, then pointed proudly to a sepia photograph in a heavy gilt frame hanging by the door.

"That wer' Jack. Had that taken in Salop he did. Not long ' fore he were killed". The landlord fell silent for a moment.

"Course 'fore the War, years ago mind, I were in the Territorials. Mind yer, I were nowt more than a lad. Had to give it up of course, what with this damn' leg. Had more hair then too." As if to emphasise the fact, he ran his hand over the top of his head, and laughed.

We chatted about this and that for upwards of ten minutes, while the landlord busied himself swilling out tankards in the stone sink behind the bar. I learnt that both he and his wife had only but recently taken the place over. Himself, he'd been born at Lydbury North, over on the Walcot Estate. Before the War, he'd done a variety of jobs. Then his brother Albert had offered him a situation. Albert it transpired held the licence of the Radnor Arms, over Presteigne way. Perhaps I knew of it? I shook my head.

Anyway he'd been working for his brother for just over twelve months, learning the trade, when this place had come up for rent. Albert knew the agent, and as he and his missus had some money saved up, leastways enough to pay the rent for the next couple of years, so here they were. In fact, if things worked out, he was hoping he might even be able to buy the place.

We carried on chatting, and during the conversation, the landlord asked me what kind of day I'd had, tramping round the hills. I told him, ending up with an account of my visit to the deserted manor house, which according to the landlord was up for sale, and indeed had been for some time.

"How long's it been empty?" I asked.

"Quite a while. Can't say as how long."

"It must need quite a lot doing to it."

"Expect it does."

"Is there any land attached to it?"

"There were."

"Much?"

"Nowt but a few acres now."

"But ..."

"Most of the land's either rented out, or bin sold off. What's for sale is what yer saw."

*Whistle . . .*

Maybe it was just my imagination, but all of a sudden, the landlord seemed disinclined to continue our conversation, reluctant even to meet my eye. The atmosphere became distinctly chilly. From being rather talkative, his replies to my questions became suddenly guarded, undaunted, I persisted.

"Who owns it then?"

"Belongs to the Maitland estate. Sir James Maitland. Him that lives down near Leominster - Moreton Court."

"I see."

He had his back to me, adding up some figures.

"I suppose it's a bit isolated, the house I mean."

"Tis that."

He began drying another glass.

"No-one else live nearby?"

"Nearest farm, that be a good five or six mile away, over t'ward Leintwardine. Why d'yer ask?"

"No reason in particular. Only there was a dark haired young lad messing round about in the snow ... outside the house. I assumed he must live somewhere nearby. Either that or else he was up to no good."

The landlord whipped about, almost as if he'd been stung. He was facing me now, staring wide eyed. Beads of perspiration on his forehead. Something flickered across his face. Alarm? Apprehension? But why? For a moment he completely forgot what he was doing. A moment was all that was necessary. The glass slipped out of his hands and shattered on the stone floor behind the bar.

The sound of the breaking glass jolted him back to his senses.

"Bugger and blast, I'll get a brush."

"I'm sorry."

"Nothin' to be sorry 'bout sir. Not yer fault. I'll see if yer supper's ready."

A few moments later he came limping back, laden with both cutlery and a steaming tray bearing my supper. These he took and set down on the small table next to the settle by the fire. He must have felt some explanation was called for.

"Better for yer than sittin' at the bar."

It also, I thought, neatly precluded any further attempt at conversation on my part. In any event, a moment or two later, while the landlord was sweeping up the broken glass, the bar door opened letting in a blast of cold night air and two regulars, dressed in corduroys, leather leggings and boots, farm labourers by the look of them, came in.

Both gave me a cursory nod, then exchanged greetings with the landlord.

*. . . and I'll be there*

Whilst I applied myself to doing justice to the beef and mushroom pie and vegetables, they ordered themselves a couple of drinks. Soon all three were busily engrossed discussing the latest stock prices, and the effect the bad weather was having on farming in the county generally.

When I'd finished, I picked up my tray and set it down on the bar. I ordered myself another mug of cider.

The landlord limped off into the back kitchen to fetch my pudding. While he was gone, one of the two men standing at the bar asked me if I was staying long. I said no, and told him I was only staying the night. Providing the trains were running, I'd be on my way home to Hereford the following morning.

"Down 'ere for the week-end then?", he asked, I nodded.

"Yes" I replied, "I've been doing a bit of hill walking. Good weather for it too." The man grunted his assent.

"Whereabouts?", asked the other. He was filling a worn Broseley clay pipe with coarse black shag from out of a small battered tin.

I told them, briefly mentioning my visit to the manor house.

"Marsh Leys Hall?" This from the man with the clay pipe.

He snapped shut his tobacco tin, and thrust it deep into his pocket. The other set down his tankard sharply on the wooden surface of the bar. They eyed each other cautiously.

"Is that it's name? I'm surprised someone hasn't bought it. With some money spent on it ..."

"Estate 'll never sell that. No-one round 'ereabouts will 'ave owt to do with it."

"Why ever not ?" I asked.

But neither man seemed to have heard me. In fact, it was almost as if I had suddenly ceased to exist. The man with the pipe walked over to the fire and sat himself down in the chimney corner, where he took out a spill from the jar beside him and thrust it into the flames. His mate remained standing at the bar. Turning away from me, he wiped the froth of beer from off his lips with the back of his hand, sucked the drooping ends of his moustache, then called to his mate across the seemingly empty bar,

"Same again Sam?"

"Thanks, Bert, don't mind if I do," replied Sam. Having lit his clay pipe he got up from his seat by the hearth and resumed his place at the bar..

At that point the landlord reappeared, effectively precluding my asking any further questions. And as if to emphasise the point he set the tray with my pudding, down on the table by the fire.

*Whistle . . .*

I resumed my seat and finished my supper. While I was still eating the two men at the bar drained their tankards, bade the landlord goodnight and without further word left the inn. A moment or two later, and I saw them again, as they passed by the outside of the windows of the inn, heads bowed, caps pulled low, their hands thrust deep into their pockets, making their way down the darkened street towards Ludford Bridge.

When I'd finished eating, the landlord limped over to me and asked if there was anything else I wanted. He'd decided to close early he said, on account of the snow. Afterwards I was not so sure that was the real reason at all. But I was welcome to stay sitting by the fire for as long as I wanted. I ordered a large brandy and a pot of coffee. Picking up my tray he limped off and disappeared behind the bar.

He reappeared several minutes later with a large pot of coffee and my brandy. Setting them down on the table, he told me breakfast was served in the parlour bar any time from eight o'clock onwards the following morning. The Hereford train left at nine thirty, so I asked to have breakfast at eight.

The landlord bade me goodnight and left the bar, taking the oil lamp with him. I sat and read a couple of chapters of George Borrow's *Wild Wales* by the fire for a couple of hours. Then I extinguished the gas jets and made my way upstairs to my room.

I didn't bother to light the lamp. I undressed by the flickering light of the fire, then clambered into bed, and snuggled down between the sheets. Outside the wind had risen to almost gale force, rattling the ill-fitting casements of my window, driving sprays of sleet against the glass.

Not surprisingly it was some time before I slept, but more on account of having eaten too rich a meal somewhat later than I was wont to do, rather than the noise made by the wind. Or so I thought.

But when, eventually, I did fall asleep, I had a most unpleasant dream. Even more unnerving was the fact that the dream repeated itself with chilling regularity. I found myself in some form of low ceilinged room. I was searching for something. What, I couldn't say. Without a shadow of a doubt I knew I would prefer not to find what I was looking for, but I seemed powerless to abandon my quest.

Eventually I found what I was searching for. Something that had to be lifted up, and now I knew there was something concealed beneath it. But each time, just as I began to raise it, whatever it was, I woke up in a cold sweat.

Twice, just as I was on the point of drifting off to sleep again, I thought I heard footsteps in the passage outside my room. The second time it happened, I climbed out of bed and tiptoed to the door.

*. . . and I'll be there*

Moonlight filtered into the room through the gap in the curtains. The wind had died down, the fire had gone out. The inn seemed enveloped in a deep silence, which was somehow charged with ominous expectancy. In fact the feeling that something was about to happen became so pronounced, that I all but found myself crying out, and it was only with the greatest difficulty that I managed to control my emotions. Shivering, I stood there in my bare feet, put my ear to the door and listened intently. Nothing. Apart from the slow measured muffled ticking of the grandfather clock standing on the landing, the silence was complete. So the insistent whispering I seemed to hear in the passage outside my room must have had no existence other than in my imagination.

Eventually I made my way back to bed, struck a match, relit the oil lamp and read another chapter of my book. Then, a little after three o'clock, I turned out the lamp, snuggled down under the blankets and fell into a deep and, thankfully, dreamless sleep.

*Whistle . . .*

# Strange Meeting

Nothing further untoward occurred during the night. I was awake, up, packed and dressed the following morning well in time for the nine thirty train back to Hereford.

Of the landlord, there was no immediate sign. A maid served me my breakfast - which was excellent. Indeed the landlord remained conspicuous by his absence until shortly before I was due to leave for the station, when suddenly he reappeared. Although there was absolutely no need, he was profuse in his apologies over his absence, and trusted that everything had been to my satisfaction. During the night, he had received word that his widowed mother had been taken ill. Apparently she lived some way out of town. Owing to the bad weather it was only with the greatest difficulty that he managed to prevail upon the local doctor to attend her.

Fortunately, as things turned out it had been a false alarm. For his part the landlord seemed to have recovered something of his previous affable demeanour of the night before. Having paid my bill, I thanked him for his hospitality, and in making my farewells said I hoped his mother would continue to improve. He nodded, said that everything was now as it should be - which struck me as a singularly curious turn of phrase, and wished me a safe journey back to Hereford.

Then, with time enough to spare for the train, retracing my steps of the previous evening, I set off back across Ludford Bridge, bound for the station. I made my way up Broad Street, through the town, and down Corve Street, the bells of St Laurence's church ringing out cheerfully across the snow covered roofs of Ludlow.

Apart from myself, there was no-one else on the platform. The only member of the station staff around seemed to be the booking clerk who'd sold my ticket to me. Wisely, he chose to stay snug and warm inside his wooden panelled office.

I walked out onto the platform. Above me, just beneath the canopy, a robin was flying back and forth in search of food. It had built its nest in one of the cast iron spandrels. Crossing over the line by the footbridge, I made for the Gentlemens' Waiting Room.

As it turned out, I had a cold wait ahead of me. Someone had made an attempt to shovel away the worst of the snow from round the door of the Waiting Room, but rather perversely I thought, no-one had bothered to see to the fire inside. So

*. . . and I'll be there*

instead I stood on the snow bound platform, stamped my feet, and awaited the arrival of the Hereford train.

A short while later, below the edge of the platform, I heard the rattle of signal wires. Then with a clatter, the arm of the lower quadrant signal at the far end of the platform by the bridge, dropped to clear. In the distance, towards Craven Arms and Stokesay, a whistle sounded. Fortunately, for once, the train was on time.

Shortly afterwards, wreathed in steam, brakes squealing, the roofs of its carriages covered by a heavy layer of snow, my train drew in alongside the platform. Climbing into an empty third class compartment in the second coach, I slammed the door shut behind me, shoved up the window, and heaved my rucksack into the luggage rack opposite me. Then, taking a seat facing the engine, I settled myself back against the hard unyielding upholstery.

Up until the last minute I thought I'd have the compartment to myself. But then, just as the whistle sounded, the guard opened the door, letting in a blast of cold air, which eddied round the damp grimy compartment.

"Beggin' your pardon sir, I thought that young lad wanted to get on. Standing right by this door he was. Seems to have run off. Sorry to have troubled you sir." The guard slammed the door shut.

I heard him call "Right away," which was followed in quick succession by a shrill answering blast on the engine's whistle, and a deafening roar as the driver opened the steam cocks. A moment or two later and the three coach train was in motion, chugging noisily out of the station, shrouded in a cloud of steam and smoke, next stop Woofferton Junction, and then all stations south to Hereford.

The train soon picked up speed, the snowdrifts alongside the line sparkling in the early morning sunlight. The air was both clear and still; the sky once again a brilliant blue. Away to my left the snow shrouded bulk of Titterstone Clee reared its head above the surrounding countryside. I sat and gazed out of the window at the silent snow covered fields, across which echoed the laboured exhaust beat of the engine.

Here and there farmers were out and about in the fields putting down fodder for their livestock. Trails of smoke drifted languidly up into the clear morning air from the chimneys of isolated farms and cottages, and the houses alongside the line. From time to time, the sound of church bells echoed across the frozen landscape.

I mention these things to assure you that I was in a perfectly calm and reasonable state of mind. I'd just spent a delightful weekend in and around Ludlow. And after all, what could be more prosaic, more normal than a short cross country train journey?

*Whistle . . .*

I knew this particular stretch of line well, having travelled it many times in the past to visit an elderly cousin living in Shrewsbury, and more recently with Claire.

Since our engagement we had spent many delightful weekends together exploring the countryside of south Shropshire, visiting such quaint out-of-the-way places as Bishop's Castle, Clun with its medieval bridge and the scant remains of its Norman castle, and Clee St. Margaret, high up on the slopes of Brown Clee, with a fast flowing brook running down the length of its main street.

By now the train was already slowing down for its next stop, at Woofferton. As it clattered over the points, the carriages swaying from side to side, I made out the branch line curving in from the east. The train drew slowly to a stop alongside the platform.

Through the grimy carriage window I caught sight of the station nameboard: "Woofferton Junction: Change here for the Tenbury Wells and Bewdley Branch". As we pulled into the station, the branch train was already in the bay platform, its engine impatiently blowing off steam, awaiting both our arrival and that of the train for Shrewsbury.

Outside my compartment window, there was a great deal of coming and going on the slush covered platform: a stream of passengers getting on and off the train, doors opening and shutting, parcels being unloaded, and in the midst of all the confusion someone dropped a heavy wicker basket containing racing pigeons.

"Mind what yer doin' with my bliddy pigeons?", yelled an irate voice.

"Put that down Edwin. How many times have I told you not to do that?"

"Mrs Butterworth? Pleased to meet you."

"Is this the Bewdley train?" queried a woman's voice.

"Shrewsbury train sir? Platform 1. Over the footbridge."

I was concentrating so much on the pantomime unfolding outside the carriage window that I didn't hear the Shrewsbury train come in. I glanced up and suddenly there it was, standing in the adjacent platform.

All of a sudden, I coughed and spluttered. A dense fug of steam and smoke was swirling about in the narrow space between the two trains, strands of which eddied in through the half open window on the far side of my compartment. And yet I could distinctly remember closing the window before the train left Ludlow. I could only assume it must have slipped open when the carriage lurched passing over the points at the north end of the station.

I stood up, crossed the few feet to the door of the carriage, and grasping hold of the leather strap began pulling up the window. As I did so, instinctively I looked across into the compartment of the Shrewsbury train standing opposite.

*. . . and I'll be there*

It was empty, or so I thought. Then suddenly, through the haze of smoke and steam, there he was. A slight, dark haired lad, bearing an uncanny resemblance to the young boy I'd seen at the manor house the previous afternoon, standing motionless, his pale face pressed against the misted glass of the carriage window. We were so close, that I felt if I'd let down the window, I could have reached out and touched him.

The hubbub on the platform outside my compartment faded into silence. Time seemed to stand still. Then somewhere, seemingly a long way off, a whistle sounded. There was a sudden jolt and my train began to move slowly out of the station.

I shoved up the window and sat down in my seat. For some unaccountable reason, I was shivering. But why should the mere sight of a boy who I hadn't seen before, or even if I had, have such an effect upon me? It didn't make any sense. None of it did.

The train was picking up speed again now, next stop Berrington and Eye, then Leominster. A lingering wisp of steam drifted about the ceiling of the carriage. For a moment or two I followed its course, as it wafted back and forth across the cheerless compartment, until at last it dissipated into thin air.

What I saw next, made me sit bolt upright on my seat. On the wall opposite me, just below where the mesh of the luggage rack sagged beneath the weight of my rucksack, were two framed prints. One was a view of Shrewsbury, looking across the Severn towards the town from the English Bridge; what the other one was, I cannot now recall.

Between the prints was a mirror, its surface deeply pitted, on which some of the steam had condensed. Nothing out of the ordinary in that, except that scrawled in the condensation, in large letters, such as a child might write, were the words:
*"Help me, plcase."*

I rubbed my eyes in amazement. But when I looked again at the mirror, the condensation had all but evaporated. And of the letters themselves, there was no trace. None whatsoever.

The remainder of my journey down to Hereford, and indeed the rest of that Sunday, passed off without any further incident. Claire was there to meet me at Barrs Court station and we had a very passable lunch in a little restaurant not far from the Eign Gate. I said nothing to her about what had occurred, and if she found me somewhat reticent, she made no comment.

We spent the rest of the short winter's day strolling along the banks of the Wye, before I saw Claire home and returned to my rooms later that same afternoon.

*Whistle . . .*

# Leases and a Letter

Back in Hereford, the following Monday I returned to work, bright and early at my firm of solicitors, Evans, Chapman and Jenkins. My chambers lay just off Church Street, in the shadow of the cathedral.

On my return, both Ferguson and Matthews, together with several other of my colleagues asked me how my week-end had gone. I told them. At least, I told them as much as I felt able to tell them.

I spent most of that morning working my way through the seemingly endless clauses of several leases, concerning myself with easements, restrictive covenants and a whole host of other legal minutiae, most of which were extremely tedious. So much so that I had little time to reflect on what had occurred over the week-end.

From time to time I glanced out of the window, across the Close towards the cathedral. Just outside the north porch a group of boys from the Cathedral School were larking about in the snow. One of them was being rolled around on the ground by his fellows.

I heard the cathedral clock striking eleven. Shortly afterwards there was a light tap at my door, and Wickin, the junior clerk, brought me in tea and toast.

I was so engrossed in what I was doing that I didn't pay him much attention. In any event, I didn't care for him much. He was far too obsequious for my liking, with lank greasy hair and dark shifty eyes. When I first met him, he reminded me instantly of Uriah Heep in Dickens' *David Copperfield*, and his subsequent manner did nothing to dispel my first impression.

He wore a perpetually miserable expression on his sallow face and seemed to suffer from a permanent cold. I often thought Wickin would have been far better employed as a professional mourner. I felt he would look excellent in a top hat and black frock coat following the hearse, at a suitably discreet distance of course.

He enquired if my visit to Bartholomew and Abney in London during the previous week had brought the matter in question any closer to a successful resolution. I told him we awaited further developments. He then proceeded to inform me that whilst I was away there had been a great deal of excitement here in the Close. Apparently, sometime during the latter part of last week a young boy had disappeared from the Cathedral School. It was rumoured he'd been seen talking to a soldier, shortly before he vanished, although it was unclear whether or not the latter was involved in the boy's disappearance.

*. . . and I'll be there*

In order to try and trace the boy, and indeed the soldier, the authorities, by which I assumed Wickin meant the local constabulary, had been making extensive enquiries in the city. Including round the Close. Even here.

Wickin seemed more appalled by the visit paid by members of the constabulary to our chambers, than by the fact that a young boy was missing. No doubt because such a visitation would have caused him to have to bestir himself somewhat more than on occasion he was wont to do.

"Well, I hope they find the boy soon," I said.

Wickin said nothing. He seemed not to have heard me. Instead he was looking out of the window and he sniffed audibly.

"Shouldn't be allowed."

"Pardon?" I queried.

"Shouldn't be allowed." he repeated and sniffed again.

"What shouldn't be allowed?"

"Those boys, playing there. It's hallowed ground. It's..." He paused, groping for a word to convey his outrage. "It's disrespectful, most disrespectful. I shall speak to the Headmaster."

I went and stood by the window looking out.

"Well they're not doing any harm. Anyway that one's had enough already". I pointed out one of the boys, a dark haired young lad, who'd taken himself off and sat himself down on one of the stone seats just inside the north porch.

"I'm sure you did just the same when you were a boy."

On reflection I was not sure of any such thing. Wickin had probably been born miserable. He sniffed again.

"These papers arrived for you sir, by the second post." With another sniff, and a backward contemptuous glance out of the window, Wickin took himself off and left me to my work.

I glanced briefly at the package. It bore a Leominster postmark and was correctly addressed to our chambers. In fact it would have been unremarkable, had it not been for one small detail. Whoever had marked it down for my attention, had been someone other than the person who had written the remainder of the address. The writing was completely different. I put the package aside, sat down, and continued working steadily through the remaining clauses of the leases until lunchtime.

About twelve thirty there was another knock at my door. It was Wickin. He sniffed and glanced out of the window. I followed his gaze and smiled. The boys had gone and outside it was getting foggy.

*Whistle . . .*

He was, he said, collecting our orders for luncheon from the Wig and Pen, which stood on the corner of Church Street and the passageway leading to our chambers. As if to reinforce what he said, he indicated the large empty wicker basket which he was carrying on his arm. I asked him to fetch me a beef pie, gravy, mashed potatoes and vegetables.

After he'd gone, I glanced out of the window again. Already the vast bulk of the cathedral had all but disappeared, hidden from sight by the ever creeping fog. It seemed to be growing denser by the minute. Indeed, it became so dark in my room, that after lunch I was compelled to light the lamp on my desk. That done, I carried on working my way through the final clauses of the last of the leases.

By about three o'clock I'd finished. I stood up and wandered over to the window. Outside, the fog was thicker than ever. Below me, down in the silent snow covered Close, I made out the dim form of the lamp lighter. Not surprisingly, on this foggy December afternoon, he was doing his rounds early.

Just after that, Wickin knocked on the door again and brought in my tea. Having seen to the fire in my room, he was on his way out, when suddenly he paused in the open doorway and turned round.

"Excuse me asking sir, but you haven't forgotten those papers, sir, the ones I brought you in this morning?" he sniffed.

"Thankyou Wickin. No, I hadn't forgotten."

I had, but I saw no reason to tell him so.

After he'd gone out, I went and sat down at my desk.

Picking up the package, I slit it open and took out what was inside. A letter enclosing a thick wad of documents from a local firm of solicitors in Leominster. Despite the fact the papers were marked for my attention, I'd never heard of them before - Wynn, Williams and Wynn of Bull Yard, Etnam Street, Leominster, Herefordshire.

I unfolded the letter and read as follows:-

*Dear Sirs,*
*Re Captain Edward James Maitland (deceased)*
*We respectfully beg to inform you that we are instructed by the next-of-kin and act as executors in the settlement of the estate of the afore-mentioned Captain Edward James Maitland late of Lower Moreton Court, Herefordshire...*

I turned the page.

*... and of Marsh Leys Hall, near Ludlow in the County of Shropshire.*

*We are given to understand that certain papers, appertaining to the estate of the deceased, are presently in the possession of your goodselves, in connection with, amongst other matters, property situate within the City of Hereford.*

*We would be obliged if you would forward those papers to ourselves at your earliest convenience, to enable us to expedite the settlement of this matter.*

*We remain Sirs,*

*for Wynn, Williams and Wynn.*

*Solicitors and Commissioners for Oaths.*

Not surprisingly, I couldn't read the signature.

Coincidence? I thought not. Suddenly the room seemed to have grown very hot and stuffy. Beads of perspiration started on my forehead. I sat back in my chair and loosened my tie. I felt desperately in need of some fresh air.

I stood up, donned my outer clothes, opened the door and walked down the passage leading to the tiny room, just off the outer lobby, where Wickin sat perched on a stool, hunched over his desk, busily scratching away in a ledger.

"Bob Cratchit," I thought, somewhat uncharitably.

As I entered the room, Wickin left off what he was doing and stood up.

"If Mr Chapman asks for me, would you tell him I've just stepped outside for a while to get some fresh air. I've got the most awful headache. Probably concentrating too much on those damn' leases this morning."

He sniffed. "Yes sir. Certainly sir."

I could never quite make up my mind if his studied politeness was for real or part of an elaborate pretence. For all I knew he probably had wax effigies of each of us stuffed full of pins lying in a draw at his lodgings.

*Whistle...*

# Bishop Stanbury's Chantry

I opened the outer door, made my way down the wooden staircase, and out into the cold murk of the foggy December afternoon. Outside it was bitterly cold. A piercing, biting cold. The fog swirled eerily about me and it was thicker than ever. A real peasouper.

I desperately needed somewhere quiet to sit and collect my thoughts. I found myself making my way along the snow covered pavement, which led across the Close towards the north door of the cathedral. "Well," I thought, "why not?" The cathedral was as good a place as any.

The upper reaches of the central tower were lost to sight beneath the dense swirling blanket of fog. Stopping briefly under one of the lamps in the Close, I pulled out my watch. It was nearly four o'clock. Good, there was time enough. Evensong wasn't until five. Taking off my hat, I walked in under the north porch, descended a couple of worn steps and pushed open the inner door of the small wooden vestibule.

Inside the cathedral it was already quite dark, but surprisingly warm, owing to the presence of a large cast iron stove which stood by the door, radiating hot air into the soaring darkness but, oddly enough, the need I'd felt for fresh air, when in my chambers but a short time ago, had passed. Now I felt chilled to the bone. So, for a few minutes I stood and warmed my gloved hands on the pipes of the stove.

After a while I felt somewhat better. Slowly I began to walk down the north aisle of the nave, past the monument to Bishop Booth, all but hidden from view behind its iron railings, towards the north transept, my footsteps echoing noisily on the flagstones. There was no-one else about, I had the building to myself.

Apart from the four tall lighted candles, set round the shrine of Bishop Thomas Cantelupe, the north transept was in total darkness. Maybe it was just my imagination, but as I crossed the transept and carried on up the north aisle of the chancel, I had the oddest feeling that someone was following me, keeping pace with my every step.

Whoever it was took care to remain just out of sight, either behind one of the stone pillars in the nave or the wooden stalls of the choir. A verger ? Hardly. Somehow I couldn't imagine a verger, let alone any other member of the cathedral clergy behaving in such a childish manner. It was probably one of the boys from the Cathedral School.

*. . . and I'll be there*

"Alright," I thought, "two can play that kind of game." Suddenly I stopped dead in my tracks and spun round. But the moment I did so, the feeling of being followed vanished. I must confess I felt a little foolish, and yet, for all that, I could not shake off the uncomfortable impression that somehow, I was not alone after all. Beyond me, the massive stone arches of the nave stretched away into the darkness, streaked with confusing, shifting, somehow menacing shadows. Despite the silence, the cathedral seemed filled with all manner of movement - muffled footsteps and hushed whisperings, so much so that I found myself shivering. Undaunted, I called out.

"Is there someone there?"

"Shades of *The Listeners*", I thought, and like the traveller knocking on the moonlit door, not surprisingly I received no reply. My voice echoed and re-echoed round the walls of the vast empty building. I stood still and listened for the slightest sound or movement. There was none. The silence was complete, and yet ...

I turned on my heel and walked on. A few moments later I found myself by the doorway leading to the beautiful chantry chapel built for Bishop Stanbury in the fifteenth century, and now set aside for private prayer. Ducking under the low doorway, I walked into the little chapel and sat down beneath the ornately carved stone ceiling on one of the plain rush seated chairs. I sat there for a long time, lost in thought. Except for the small red votive light, hanging in front of the altar, the chapel was in total darkness.

My odd experiences of the last few days seemed to have begun with my visit to the manor house. But what did they really amount to?

I told myself any building, if it remained empty long enough, was likely to attract the attentions of local children.

When I was a boy growing up in Market Drayton, there was just such a place. The house, now long since demolished, I forget its name, stood on the edge of the town. Together with my cousins Robert and Samuel, I used to clamber over the surrounding brick wall and play in the overgrown gardens. We built ourselves a hideout in the derelict coach-house. We even broke a few of the windows.

There were all kinds of stories as to why the house remained empty, most of the more lurid ones made up by ourselves to scare away the other children.

The footsteps? The landlord's explanation seemed far more likely. As if to confirm my thoughts, at that precise moment, somewhere in the darkness of the empty cathedral, a board creaked.

My dream? Well, what of it? I'd had unpleasant dreams before, though admittedly I couldn't recall having had one that occurred over and over again.

*Whistle . . .*

As for the boy on the train? I couldn't even be sure he was the same one I'd seen at the manor house on the previous day. And even if he was, what of it?

As to the writing on the mirror? It probably had been made by a child - earlier in the day - only to reveal itself when the steam condensed on the mirror.

The package from, what was their name? Ah, yes, Messrs. Wynn, Williams and Wynn in Leominster. Well, that was odd. A coincidence, but nothing more than that.

After that little exorcism, I felt much better. A few moments later, I stood up and as I did so, I heard something metallic drop onto the chapel floor. "Damn," I thought. "One of my cufflinks." They'd been a birthday present from Claire earlier in the year. She'd even gone to the expense of having them engraved with my initials. I had to find it.

Taking off my gloves, I knelt down on the cold stone floor of the chapel and cast about with my hands, until they closed on something small and metallic. It was only when I stood up again, that I realised both my links were still fast in the cuffs of my shirt.

I opened the palm of my hand. In it lay what looked like a small medallion, though in the darkness I couldn't really be sure what it was. It was about the size of a St Christopher. I slipped it into one of the pockets of my overcoat, intending to look at it later, picked up my hat and gloves and walked out of the chapel.

I walked back down the aisle, past the north transept and made my way towards the porch. Just as I reached the stove, for one brief moment the fingers of my right hand closed on the small medallion deep within the pocket of my overcoat. As they did so, something like a sigh slid through the darkness.

"Help me, please," said a voice just behind me. It was little more than a whisper, and yet at the same time very distinct. I spun round, and almost blundered into one of the cathedral vergers.

"Sorry if I startled you sir."

"What did you just say?", I asked somewhat curtly.

"I... asked if you were alright sir. If ... you needed any help..." His voice trailed away.

"No, I'm alright. Thankyou," I said dryly.

Donning my gloves and hat, I opened the door of the wooden vestibule and made my way out of the cathedral. Somewhere above me, lost in the fog, the cathedral clock chimed the half hour.

*. . . and I'll be there*

# Mr Chapman Makes A Request

Back in my room, I barely had time to divest myself of my outer clothes, when there was a timid knock at my door.

It was Wickin. He sniffed.

"Mr Chapman's been asking for you sir. I explained you didn't feel well and had stepped outside for a while. He asked me to tell you he'd like to see you when you got back."

"Thankyou, Wickin."

I made my way down the passage and knocked on Mr Chapman's door. A summons to the august presence of the senior partner of Evans, Chapman and Jenkins was not to be taken lightly.

"Come," said an imperious voice from within.

I opened the door and went in.

At the far end of the room, just in front of the window, Mr Chapman sat at his large mahogany desk, the surface of which was all but hidden under piles of neatly stacked papers. Outside, just beyond the uncurtained window, strands of fog eddied and swirled about in the darkness of the December afternoon.

The room itself was almost entirely lined with glass fronted oak bookshelves, filled to overflowing with leather bound copies of Law Reports, Statutes and various other legal journals. A cheerful fire burned in the small grate, the flames of which reflected in the polished glass and woodwork of the room.

"Stephen, my boy. Come in and sit down. Wickin tells me you're not well. I'd have thought you'd have blown away any cobwebs in the hills over the week-end."

Mr Chapman regarded me thoughtfully for a moment over the top of his glasses. He was a slight, elderly man of about sixty, with an alert vigour that belied his thatch of grey hair, mutton chop whiskers and a pair of beady brown eyes.

"Not working you too hard, are we? Wickin said you were having a bit of difficulty ... with some leases? Said he'd be glad to help." The corners of his mouth twitched. The ghost of a smile flickered across his face. Very little escaped Mr Chapman. "Sit down Stephen, sit down."

He motioned me to the empty leather chair in front of him on the opposite side of the desk. I sat down and gripped the arms of the chair tightly with my hands. At that point I could cheerfully have committed a serious assault on young Wickin, regardless of the consequences.

*Whistle . . .*

"No, sir. It's nothing really. I think I've just picked up a slight chill. That's all."

Mr Chapman nodded. Then, reaching forward, seemingly at random, he picked up a bundle of documents loosely tied together with a scrap of red ribbon, from off the top of one of the piles of papers. Settling back in his chair, he began to peruse them.

I sat and waited.

"What," asked Mr Chapman, without taking his eyes from the papers before him for an instant, "do you know of the Maitlands of Lower Moreton Court ?" Whilst awaiting my reply, he continued to peruse the papers in his hand.

During the three years I'd been with Evans, Chapman and Jenkins, I'd found it always paid to be frank and open with Mr Chapman. He didn't suffer fools gladly. In fact he didn't suffer them at all. That being the case, whatever it cost me later, I spoke the simple truth.

"Nothing, sir. I didn't even know they were clients of ours."

Mr Chapman nodded. Seemingly it was the answer he expected.

"Of very long standing. Though why, after all these years, Sir James should have chosen to instruct others in such a straightforward matter, I really cannot begin to understand. Can you Stephen?"

"No sir."

"Now where was I ?"

"You were telling me about the Maitlands, sir."

"Ah yes. An old county family. One can see the house from the train, Lower Moreton Court, near Leominster. I believe the estate is quite extensive, several hundred acres. Five or six farms. Good fishing and shooting too. There's also some property over the border in Shropshire, round Ludlow, or so Wickin has given me to understand."

Suddenly the atmosphere in the room seemed to have grown very hot and oppressive. I shifted round on my chair, then coughed and swallowed hard.

"Including Marsh Leys Hall sir?" I asked, desperately hoping that I'd managed somehow to contrive to keep my voice sounding normal. But if Mr Chapman noticed my discomfort, he gave no indication of it.

"Evidently," dismissively he cast the papers he was holding aside.

"And Captain Maitland?"

Normality returned.

"Went out to Canada as a young man, or so I seem to recall. Came back to England shortly after War was declared. Offered a commission in the Light Infantry, accepted. Eventually posted over to France. Awarded the Military

*. . . and I'll be there*

Cross, escorting an ammunition convoy up the Bligny road. Killed near Cambrai, a week or so before the Armistice was signed. Damned shame."

"Mind you, I didn't know him that well. My partner, Maurice Evans, knew him much better, before your time. Both dead now, they were up at Winchester together and then at 'varsity. In any event we always tended to act for the father, old Sir James. Well, at least Maurice, as the senior partner, did. I know the old man took Edward's death very hard, and after all..." Mr Chapman fell silent for a moment, seemingly lost in thought.

I sat and waited for him to continue.

"Maurice told me there'd been a difference of opinion between father and son, sometime before Edward was killed. But as for what it was about, I really have no idea. That apart, I don't think they ever patched up their differences."

"I see, Edward Maitland, he never married?"

"No."

"And the old man, sir, is he still alive?"

"Sir James Maitland? I believe so. Although he must be nearly seventy now."

"Wife?"

"Lady Frances, died just before the War."

"No other children?"

"A daughter, Rosalind, married Sir George Aubrey some years ago. Young family, they went out to India, before the War. Husband's now on the Viceroy's staff in Delhi. When Sir James dies, I suppose the entire Maitland estate will pass to her."

"Normally, I'd suggest that Waterfield or Wickin deal with the matter. But, as Sir James Maitland has been a long standing client, I think he deserves somewhat better treatment than that. After all, we wouldn't wish it to be suggested that we were any less than attentive in our final dealings with him, than in our first, now would we?"

I shook my head.

"No sir, indeed not."

"Even if Sir James has seen fit to take his business elsewhere," added Mr Chapman, with just the faintest hint of sarcasm in his voice.

"I'd deal with it myself Stephen, but as you can see, I'm rather heavily engaged just at the moment." Mr Chapman smiled, opened his hands, palms upward, and spread them expansively over his desk.

"Then of course,", he continued, "I have that matter to attend to for the Dean and Chapter. In fact, I may well find myself spending quite some time over at the Deanery during the next few days."

*Whistle . . .*

Momentarily Mr Chapman glanced out of the window, in the direction of his thoughts, towards the Deanery which lay across the Close beyond the east end of the cathedral, now lost to sight in the deep murk of the December evening.

Then, he turned back to me.

"Would you mind dealing with it yourself Stephen?"

"No, not at all sir. Although I intended asking you about it first anyway."

"Capital. Take whatever time you need, and get young Wickin to ferret out the papers. After all he offered to help you, didn't he?"

"I'll give him help," I thought. Mentally I made a note to ensure young Wickin gave me all the help I needed. He could start by fetching the Maitland papers from storage down in the cellar. That should keep him occupied for sometime.

I looked up. Mr Chapman was watching me closely through his gold rimmed pince-nez. He must have read my thoughts, as he smiled and, almost imperceptibly, nodded his head. He reached for the heavy decanter and glasses which stood on a silver tray, atop a small table alongside his desk.

"Whisky?"

"Thankyou sir."

He poured two generous fingers into the glass, then did the same for himself.

"Here you are Stephen. Get that down you. Help you chase away that cold."

Outside, across the fog shrouded Close, the cathedral clock struck five.

*. . . and I'll be there*

# An Evening's Entertainment

That evening Claire and I had booked supper at the Green Dragon Hotel in Broad Street. Afterwards we intended going on to see a performance of "Lady Windermere's Fan" by Oscar Wilde, which was playing at the Garrick Theatre up on Widemarsh Street.

I left my chambers about half past five, which gave me just enough time to head back to my rooms for a quick wash and a change of clothes, before meeting Claire at the hotel just after seven.

I walked slowly across the snow shrouded Close and out into Broad Street. Just outside the precincts of the cathedral a chestnut seller had set up his barrow, and was busy hawking his wares.

"Nice hot chestnuts, penny a bag sir."

I nodded and shook my head.

"Goodnight to you then sir."

"Goodnight."

My lodgings lay across the river, on the south side of the city. The fog was worse than ever, the street lamps burning but dimly through the murk. The surface of the pavements, often treacherous at this time of the year, were covered by a thick coating of ice, turning them into nothing short of a glacial hell for both wary and unwary alike.

Taking extreme care, amidst a constant blare of horns, the ringing of bells, the jingle of harness, the clip-clop of hooves and the rumble of wheels, I made my way slowly along Broad Street and Palace Yard, towards Gwynne Street and the Wye Bridge.

Twice, despite my vigilance, I almost lost my footing on the ice bound pavement. I was not alone in that. My fellow pedestrians, for the most part like myself, heads bowed and warmly wrapped against the freezing chill of the winter's night, slipped and slithered their way along the icy pavements, homeward bound.

Motor buses, cabs, delivery boys on their bicycles, horse drawn carts and drays laden with all manner of merchandise, coal and oil, and produce from the market, suddenly loomed up out of the fog, only to disappear just as swiftly, swallowed up by the choking murk.

A little further on, where Palace Yard merged into Gwynne Street, just by the gatehouse of the Bishop's Palace, the road menders had been at work. A pile of

*Whistle . . .*

granite sets, already rimed with frost, stood neatly stacked by the side of a deep excavation, fenced off from the rest of the street by rough wooden boards, illuminated by the brightly burning flares of naphtha lamps.

As I passed by, the night watchman, his cap pulled firmly down over his ears and heavily muffled against the biting cold, was already making himself comfortable in front of the coke filled brazier, placed just outside the entrance to his small canvas tent.

A steam wagon, heavily laden with a load of barrels from Bulmers' brewery, trundled past me, hissing and wheezing, as it made its ponderous way along the narrow street. Just as the driver slowed for the corner, suddenly a young boy darted out across the road from the other side of the street, right in front of the lumbering wagon. The driver braked hard and blew furiously on his whistle. The boy disappeared into the darkness, down a narrow fog shrouded alleyway, in the direction of the bridge. If he'd missed his footing on the slippery surface of the road, the boy wouldn't have stood a chance.

Oddly enough, it was just then that I remembered the small medallion I'd found in Bishop Stanbury's chantry. I pushed my gloved hand down deep into the pocket of my overcoat, just to make sure it was still there. Reassuringly, my hand closed on it almost immediately.

I stood to one side, while a coal cart rumbled across the ancient stone bridge, and glanced down at the fast-flowing river.

Beneath me, the normally placid waters of the Wye were in spate. Washed downstream by the winter rains, a mass of driftwood had snagged against the breakwaters on the western side of the bridge, round which the swollen waters frothed and foamed, before racing under the narrow arches, surging on their way southwards towards Chepstow, the Severn, and the sea. A chill wind rose up from off the river. If it turned much colder there might even be ice floes on the river, as there had been in previous years.

Not surprisingly, the walk back to my lodgings took me somewhat longer than usual, on account of both the fog and the snow. After about twenty minutes, I turned, thankfully, into Wye Street.

My lodgings lay on the north side of the street, at the far end of a three storey brick fronted Regency terrace. Low heavy iron railings, now all but hidden beneath a thick layer of snow, separated the small front garden from the street. A short flight of steps led up from the path to a tall porticoed entrance.

Outside the house a noisy group of rosy cheeked children were clustered round the muffin man, who, not surprisingly on this cold winter's night, was doing a

*. . . and I'll be there*

roaring trade. At the far end of the street a snowball fight was in progress. A horse drawn pony and trap clattered past me, eventually coming to a halt at one of the houses on the opposite side of the road.

I turned in at the front gate. It stood half ajar. I pushed against it, but found it wouldn't open any further, owing to the snow which had drifted across the path behind it.

Normally I was home before the paper boy. Tonight, however, he'd beaten me to it. I could see his footprints in the snow. I made my way round the small square of garden and up the narrow, snow bound entry, which led to the rear of the house and the door to my lodgings.

Although the landlord retained the first and second floors, together with the basement, for himself and his family, my rooms were, nevertheless, spacious. In fact, I had the whole of the third floor to myself. The principal rooms, although north facing, overlooked the river. My sitting room had the best view of all. It had two tall sash windows, with window seats beneath, set either side of a pair of glass doors opening onto a small balcony, from which I could look right across to the old part of the city, tumbling its way down to the very banks of the Wye: the cathedral, the Bishop's Palace, and beyond the jumble of weathered roofs, at the far end of Broad Street, the twisted spire of All Saints' church with its massive weathercock.

Both Claire and I had spent many a long summer's evening, sitting on the balcony after supper, gazing across the tree-lined banks of the Wye to the huddle of ancient roofs and spires, while below us, swans floated past on the river. There could, I reflected, be few finer views in the whole of England.

Tonight however, all that was lost to sight, hidden beneath a dense blanket of freezing fog which had persisted throughout virtually the entire day.

I let myself in and made my way up the wooden staircase. It was only when I reached the door to my rooms that I realised that the newspaper boy, presumably in a hurry to be off, had, after all, forgotten to leave my evening paper.

Inside, the curtains had been drawn across the windows of my sitting room, the lamps lit and a cheerful fire burned in the grate. I was, I reflected, extremely fortunate in both my lodgings and my landlord. Perhaps the fact that he was also Claire's uncle had something to do with it. Hurriedly I stripped off my outer clothes, tossed them down onto the leather chair by the fire, went into the bathroom, slipped off my shirt, ran a bowl of hot water, washed and shaved.

After that, I walked into the bedroom and took out a fresh shirt from the chest of drawers. As I was putting in my cufflinks, I suddenly remembered the medallion

*Whistle...*

I'd found in the cathedral earlier that afternoon. I went back into the sitting room, slipped my hand down into the pocket of my overcoat, and pulled it out.

I took the medallion back into the bedroom, sat down on the edge of my bed, and turned up the lamp. As it happened, I'd been wrong. It wasn't a St Christopher after all. It was a military cap badge, German by the look of it. Probably a souvenir from the War, but an odd thing, nevertheless, to find in the cathedral.

For some unaccountable reason my hands began to shake as I turned it over. On the reverse was a short inscription, very lightly engraved, written in French. I held the badge up to the light to get a better look at the words. What I read, with mounting disbelief, set my heart pounding in my chest:-

A

Christopher

De Son Papa

E.J.M.

1917

"E.J.M" Edward James Maitland? I shivered. Suddenly the room seemed to have grown very cold. I felt a tingling sensation at the base of my spine. Outside, beyond my bedroom window, the sounds in the street below faded into silence.

Gently, almost reverently, I placed the cap badge down on top of the bedside table next to the lamp. I sat there on my bed, staring at it till my head ached, desperately seeking some logical reason for something I did not understand, could not explain. I felt my heart thumping against my chest. In an effort to overcome a rising tide of panic which threatened to engulf me, I dug the nails of my fingers deep into the palms of my hands. As if far off, through the open door of my bedroom, I heard the clock on the mantelpiece in the sitting room chiming the half hour.

After a while the feeling passed and I felt somewhat calmer. Slowly I stood up and somehow I managed to finish dressing. The sitting room clock struck a quarter to seven. If I was to be on time to meet Claire at the Green Dragon as arranged, I'd have to be on my way. Leaving the cap badge on the bedside table, I slipped on my outer clothes, opened the door of my rooms, and made my way downstairs.

Outside, the fog was thicker than ever. Whether it was just my nerves, the intense cold, or something else, I had the greatest difficulty in locking the outside door, and yet I'd never had any problem with it before. The lock was kept well oiled and in my frustration I ended up by dropping the key in the snow.

*. . . and I'll be there*

As I bent down to pick it up, something struck me as singularly odd about the footprints left in the snow by the newspaper boy. Exactly what, I couldn't then say. Baffled, I stood up. Once again I tried the key in the lock. This time, without any further ado, the catch slid smoothly home.

It wasn't until I was about halfway down Wye Street, that it suddenly dawned on me what was odd about the footprints. So odd, that as the realisation of it hit me, I stopped dead, almost losing my footing on the icy pavement.

The footprints led up the entry right enough, but there were none, at least none that I'd seen, leading back down to the gate. Either I'd missed seeing them in the darkness, or else the lad had taken a short cut and slipped over the garden wall. He'd done so before. I'd seen him do it. But somehow this time I knew he hadn't. If I was right about the footprints, and the lad hadn't taken a short cut, then what other possible explanation could there be?

I made my way back across the bridge and headed up King Street. There were fewer people about now. Several of the shops had already closed for the night. The grocers were already half shuttered and I glanced within. Inside, behind the heavy wooden counter, the shopkeeper was still busily engaged, weighing out a measure of tea for one last minute customer.

Outside the butchers, the boys were just beginning the nightly chore of taking down what remained of the bewildering array of game and poultry I'd seen festooning the front of the shop earlier that day on my way to work - rabbits, hares, wood pigeons, partridges, pheasants, geese, chickens and turkeys. As I passed by an open doorway a little further on up the street, a deliciously savoury smell wafted out into the cold night air, reminding me of the supper awaiting me at the Green Dragon Hotel.

It was bitterly cold, and the fog showed no sign of lifting. The night watchman was still there, snug within his little tent, wreathed in a fug of fumes from his brazier, but the chestnut seller had disappeared.

I reached the Green Dragon Hotel just after seven. Claire was already waiting for me in the entrance hall. I apologised for being slightly late, and blamed it on the pressure of work, which I suppose was not very far from the truth. Other than that, I resolved to say nothing further to Claire about what had taken place, either over the week-end or since returning to my chambers.

"Shall we go in?", I asked, offering Claire my arm.

The supper served at the Green Dragon Hotel more than justified our expectations. The roast beef was done to perfection and the wine an excellent vintage.

*Whistle . . .*

Sadly the play was not up to the same standard, but then after all, it was only an amateur production. Even so, I would have thought the actor playing Lord Augustus Lorton would have mastered his lines. As he hadn't, he missed two important cues, which caused his fellow actors several anxious moments.

The play didn't finish till half past ten, so by the time I'd escorted Claire back to her parents' house, which lay on the outskirts of the city, off White Cross Road, it was already quite late. Claire's parents were still up when we arrived back at the house, and she asked me if I'd like to step inside for a few moments, and perhaps have a nightcap with her father. But as it was already past eleven, and it was a fair step back to my lodgings, I politely declined, kissed her goodnight on the doorstep, and set off back to my rooms.

Rather than take a cab, I decided to walk. I felt the fresh air would do me good, particularly after the smoke filled atmosphere of the theatre, and, after all, I needed a clear head for the morning. I was representing a client in a contested matter in court first thing and I had to be at my best, particularly since the other side were fielding a barrister from Cabot Chambers, across the Severn, in Bristol. So, as I made my way back through the silent snowbound streets of the city, my mind was on the morrow's forthcoming case, to the exclusion of all else.

By the time I reached Wye Street, I thought I had every eventuality, every possible line of legal argument, well and truly covered. Well pleased with myself, I unlocked the door of my lodgings, and walked upstairs to my rooms.

Then I thought, as I turned out the lamps in the sitting room and made my way into the bedroom, while I'm in court tomorrow morning, young Wickin can use his time profitably for once, and ferret out those papers for me from down in the cellar.

*. . . and I'll be there*

# Echoes from the Past

The following morning I was up bright and early, washed, shaved, dressed, breakfasted, and on my way to my chambers to collect my brief, well before nine o'clock. My mood matched the day. Above me the sky was a peerless blue, with not a cloud in sight. Although it was still bitterly cold, overnight, the fog had lifted, and the sun had come out. Indeed, the only cloud on the horizon, if it could be called that, was the disappearance of the cap badge, although I felt sure its loss was only temporary.

Yet I was certain I'd put it down on my bedside table the previous night, shortly before I went out to meet Claire at the Green Dragon Hotel. But this morning when I came to look for it not half an hour since, just before I left my lodgings, the badge had disappeared. I thought I might have knocked it off the bedside table during the night. But a quick search round the floor of my bedroom on my hands and knees revealed nothing.

However, as Claire would confirm, I was in the habit of putting things away for safe keeping, then not being able to find them again afterwards. No matter. The badge would turn up again sooner or later. After all, it had to be somewhere in my rooms.

I was annoyed with myself for not taking better care of it. I'd intended taking the badge into the man who kept the small shop dealing in coins and medals in High Town, not far from the Market Hall, whom of all people, I thought, most likely to be able to tell me the badge's provenance.

I carried on walking, crunching across the hard packed snow covering the cathedral Close, in the direction of Church Street. Indeed, I was almost within sight of my chambers, thinking about nothing in particular, when suddenly I remembered I'd forgotten to take another look at the footprints in the entry leading to my lodgings.

Just at that precise moment, someone hailed me from across the other side of the Close - William Ferguson, a fellow solicitor from my chambers, and all thoughts of the missing cap badge, not to mention footprints, went completely out of my mind.

I duly collected my brief, leaving instructions that when Wickin arrived, whatever else he did, I required the Maitland papers on my desk by the time I returned from court.

*Whistle . . .*

In the event, that turned out to be sooner rather than later, the trial judge being indisposed with influenza, and all cases he was due to hear, being put off till the morrow, if not until next week. So, for the time being at least, all my meticulous preparations of the preceding days, not to mention last night, came to nought.

Just after eleven o'clock, I returned to my chambers, where Wickin buttonholed me in the outer lobby.

"Good morning sir. You're back early. I've found the papers you requested. They're waiting for you on your desk." He sniffed.

"Thankyou, Wickin. Perhaps you'd be so good as to put these away for me," I said, handing him the bundle of papers from the morning's court.

"And when you've done that, would you kindly draft a reply to Wynn, Williams and Wynn, the solicitors in Leominster, advising we are in receipt of their letter, and that we will write again, once matters have been resolved here."

"Yes sir. Of course sir." He sniffed audibly. "May I ask their address?"

"Bull Yard, I believe. The letter's somewhere on my desk," I said, somewhat distractedly.

"Thankyou sir."

I headed off back to my room, which lay on the other side of the building, round the corner and at the far end of a narrow passage.

Not surprisingly, given the site it occupied, right in the heart of the city, overlooking the cathedral, the building housing our chambers was extremely old. A veritable rabbit warren of a place, with all kinds of unexpected nooks and crannies, odd shaped rooms, and floors sloping at improbable angles.

I was halfway down the passage leading to my room, when suddenly I found myself stepping to one side, as one would in order to let someone pass by on their way towards the outer lobby. Yet apart from myself, there was no-one else in the passage. Not another living soul.

I told myself I must have missed my footing on the uneven floorboards and thought no more about it. In any event, a moment or two later and I was turning the brass knob of the door to my room.

For some inexplicable reason, as I opened the door I had the oddest feeling that someone had been in the room but a moment or two before my arrival - which, unless whoever it was had left by the window, was frankly impossible.

I paused in the doorway and looked slowly round the room, which of course was empty. Everything was in its usual place - chair, desk, my papers from yesterday, even down to the bright warm fire burning in the grate. As for the window, one glance told me, it was shut fast.

*. . . and I'll be there*

"Ridiculous" I said out aloud. Stepping inside, I closed the door, took off my hat and gloves, hung up my overcoat and muffler, and walked over to my desk.

On it sat an old, battered black metal dispatch box, stuck to the top of which was a scrap of paper, now yellowed with age, upon which, written in faded copperplate, were the words:-

*Papers of Captain Edward James Maitland, Lower Moreton Court, Herefordshire,* to which someone had added in a later hand, *deposited December 3rd 1917.*

On my desk, by the side of the box, lay a large, dog eared luggage label, tied to which was a small key. I sat down, picked up the key, inserted it into the lock, turned it, and lifted up the lid. Inside the dispatch box were several documents. These I took out, and for the moment at least, put to one side. Beneath them lay three faded sepia photographs.

I picked up one at random. It showed a young, dark haired woman, dressed in what must have been the height of fashion just before the Great War. I turned it over. Written on the back, in a firm round script, were the words: *December 1905* and printed at the bottom *Imprimé à Paris par G Brissot, 12 Rue de la République, France.*

The next photograph showed the same woman, elegantly attired as before, and a young English army officer, smartly turned out in what I took to be full dress uniform. On the reverse, written in the same bold script, were the words *Winchester, August 1914.*

The third photograph was of a young dark haired boy, smartly dressed in a school uniform, holding a boater. I thought it likely the photograph had been taken at the same time as the one of the army officer and the young dark haired woman.

Despite the fire in my room, suddenly it seemed to have grown very cold. I shivered, and felt a pricking sensation in the hairs on the nape of my neck.

I stood up, and took the photograph of the young boy over to the window where the light was better. For several minutes I studied it intently. But was he the same boy I'd seen at the manor house and on the train?

Then, just at that moment, two things happened together. A slight murmur slid round the walls of my room. The sound was gone in an instant. So quickly in fact, that afterwards I couldn't be certain I'd even heard it. Next to me, the sashes of the window rattled noisily in their casements. Outside, just below the window, the bare

*Whistle . . .*

branches of the lime tree in the snow covered yard, stirred slightly in the faintest of breezes.

"Christopher Maitland, I presume?" I said very softly. I turned the photograph over. But if it was confirmation I was seeking, I was in for a disappointment.

On the back of the photograph, in a different hand, was written the single word *Hereford*. But apart from that one word, there was nothing else. Not even a date.

The writing seemed strangely familiar, in particular the way the 'H' was written. For some reason I happened to glance at my desk. Lying on it was the envelope from the solicitors in Leominster. Wickin should have disposed of it. I walked over, picked it up, intending to throw it into the fire.

As I did so I happened to catch sight of that part of the address marking its contents for my attention. I took it with me, and went and stood back by the window: the envelope in one hand, the photograph of the boy in the other.

Even to my untrained eye, the words *For the attention of Stephen Harris esq.*, on the envelope, and *Hereford* on the back of the photograph, looked as though they'd been written by the same hand. That was clearly impossible. They were, nevertheless, remarkably similar.

Screwing up the envelope, I tossed it neatly into the fire, and went back and sat down at my desk. Putting the photographs aside, I began a careful examination of the rest of the contents of the dispatch box.

There were several neatly folded sheets of white paper, listing details of the numerous investments made by Captain Maitland in the years immediately preceding the outbreak of the War. Most of the investments were on a modest scale, the majority of them being in companies in both Canada and North America. It was then I recalled my conversation of the previous day with Mr Chapman, and him telling me that as a young man Edward Maitland had gone out to Canada.

I was familiar with some of the companies mentioned, Lloyds, the White Star Line and the Canadian Pacific Railway. But, the Hudson Bay Company apart, some of the Canadian concerns referred to in the papers, such as the Manitoba Electric and Gas Light Company, I'd never even heard of. Evidently Edward had been a wealthy young man, of independent means. But bearing in mind what Mr Chapman had told me about the Maitland family, that came as no surprise.

The next document I picked up was more interesting, at least from a local point of view. A long lease, commencing in July 1917, taken out by Captain Maitland himself, on a property here in Hereford - Oakfield House. I couldn't place the address. The lease still had some time to run. Attached to it was a map showing

*. . . and I'll be there*

part of the city, upon which the relevant property was shaded in pink. It lay on the north side of Hereford, on Venns Road, off Aylestone Hill.

Beneath the lease lay a bundle of letters, neatly tied together with a scrap of red ribbon. They were in French, dating from the years 1905-1906, written, I assumed, to Edward. The envelopes had not survived. The letters all began with *Mon cher* or *Mon cher Edouard*, and had been written from several different addresses in and around the Montmartre district of Paris. The writer simply signed herself *M* - presumably the young woman in the photographs, though of course of that I could not be sure. I didn't read all the letters, nor attempt a full translation of those that I did, but reading between the lines, they told a not unfamiliar tale.

A dalliance abroad, between a young Englishman footloose and fancy-free, and a pretty French girl he'd met while sightseeing in Paris.

The result of which was the birth of a child - a boy, Christopher James, born September 6th 1906 at 15 Rue des Cordeliers, Montmartre, Paris.

From the outset, it seemed clear that Edward accepted he was the boy's father, and, from the last of the letters in the bundle, Edward proposed making arrangements for both Christopher and his mother to come over to live in England - in Hereford I assumed, hence the lease on the house.

After all, it was but a short train journey and a ride in a pony and trap from the family estate at Lower Moreton Court.

Yet Mr Chapman had told me Edward Maitland never married. Perhaps he hadn't. Was his affair with the pretty French girl from Montmartre, and the subsequent birth of his son, the cause of the rift between Edward and his own father? It was possible. But again I couldn't be sure. After all, I had no way of finding out. Nor indeed any reason to do so.

Even so, I couldn't account for the ten, in fact nearly eleven, years which had elapsed between Christopher's birth in September 1906, and July 1917, when his father took out the lease on the house here in Hereford.

I wondered if Edward had been waiting to see if his father would come to terms with the situation. It was possible, but once again, I couldn't be certain, and after all, what did it matter now?

But if *M* was the child's mother, Edward his father, then the boy in the photograph must surely be young Christopher. For who else could he be? The younger brother of the woman in the other photographs? Perhaps, there was a passing resemblance, but nothing more than that. I picked up the photograph, studied it again for a moment, then laid it aside.

*Whistle . . .*

The final document in the dispatch box was a Last Will and Testament, of Captain Edward James Maitland, formerly of Lower Moreton Court, Herefordshire, England, and now of 12 Rue des Carmelites, Quebec City, Province of Quebec, Dominion of Canada.

Slowly, I turned over the crisp white pages, until I reached the last one. I glanced down it, almost to the foot of the page.

The Will was dated July 1917, and had been drawn up by a firm of solicitors in Southampton, apparently at very short notice. It looked very much as though Edward had taken the opportunity afforded him, by a spot of unexpected home leave, to make a Will. I thought unexpected, because why else had he chosen to employ a firm of solicitors down in Hampshire, rather than our own chambers? After all Mr Chapman had told me that most, if not all, of Edward's family's legal matters, his own included, had been transacted through Evans, Chapman and Jenkins here in Hereford.

Enclosed with the Will were two letters, one dated some three months later, written from Arras in northern France, in Edward's own hand, addressed to those he had but recently instructed, thanking them for expediting the drawing up of the document now before me, and asking that it be forwarded on to our own chambers.

The second letter, in fact no more than a brief note, was from the solicitors in Southampton, written to my own chambers, enclosing Edward's Last Will and Testament, apologising for the delay in forwarding it to us, but shedding no further light on why Edward had chosen to employ them.

But whatever lay behind Edward's choice of solicitors, I thought it a wise precaution on his part to have drawn up a Will. Especially in light of what I now knew about his own particular domestic circumstances, and, as it turned out, sadly prophetic. I turned back to the beginning, and began to read slowly through the various clauses and bequests.

I must have been about halfway through, when, just as the cathedral clock began to strike twelve, there was a light tap at my door. It was Wickin, enquiring whether or not I required anything for luncheon. I told him I would get something for myself in town later on.

"Oh, by the way sir," he sniffed.

"Yes, Wickin?" I was not in the mood for his non sequiturs.

"I've drafted out the letter you requested sir. Do you wish to see it, before it is despatched?"

"No, Wickin, I'm sure it will be in order."

"Very good sir."

*. . . and I'll be there*

"Thankyou Wickin."

He sniffed again and went out into the passage, closing the door behind him.

I carried on reading through the Will. Bearing in mind the enmity which Mr Chapman had told me existed between Edward and his father, the content of the document before me would, I thought, have done little towards effecting a reconciliation between the parties. Even had both so desired it.

Reaching the end of the Will, I laid it down on my desk and sat back in my chair. It was, after all, as wills go, I reflected, remarkably straightforward.

Apart from monies set aside to pay for the boy's schooling - presumably here in Hereford (that at least explained one of the photographs) - on his death Edward's entire estate was to pass to his son Christopher. I doubted very much if old Sir James would have approved of Edward's course of action. Did he, I wondered idly, even know of his grandson's existence?

I'd half expected somewhere to find out the identity of the young French woman in the other two photographs, whom I'd decided must after all be one and the same with the unknown *M* who'd written the letters to Edward.

But in that too, I was to be disappointed. There was no mention of her whatsoever. I wondered if her relationship with Edward had soured. Perhaps had not survived the outbreak of the War, and she'd gone back to France, taking Christopher with her. But again that was pure speculation on my part, and in any event, if she had, why then had Edward made provision for Christopher's schooling?

At the foot of the very last page, beneath Edward's own signature, were the names of two witnesses. The first was that of Greville Courtenay, the solicitor who had drawn up the document. The second, rather surprisingly I thought, was that of a lance corporal, in the Light Infantry, which, from what Mr Chapman had told me, I remembered had been Edward's own regiment.

The signature was smudged and unreadable. I studied it intently for several minutes, but try as I might, I couldn't make it out, but underneath it was an address. An address I knew all too well.

*West Lodge, Marsh Leys Hall, Ludlow, Shropshire.*

Outside, across the Close, the cathedral clock chimed the half hour. Time I had something to eat so I picked up the Will, gathered up the sheets containing the details of Edward's investments, and together with the photographs and the letters, dropped them all back into the empty dispatch box. As I did so, there was a faint metallic clink. I'd been mistaken, the box wasn't empty after all.

Reaching inside beneath the papers, I felt around with my fingers. A moment or two later they closed on something small and metallic. Some sixth sense told me what it was, even before I laid eyes on it. Grasping hold of it, I lifted it out of the box. There, in the palm of my hand, lay a small military cap badge.

As I turned it over, my hands were shaking, for I knew what I would find. This time, though I could have wished it otherwise, I was not mistaken.

A
Christopher
De Son Papa
E.J.M.
1917

*. . . and I'll be there*

# The Tenant of Oakfield House

Undoubtedly it was the same badge I'd found in the cathedral, which I'd mislaid somewhere in my rooms the previous night. So how on earth did it come to be here in the dispatch box ? There was no rational explanation I could offer, capable of allaying the mounting sense of fear which threatened to overwhelm me. The atmosphere in my room was stifling, the air heavy and oppressive, pressing down on me, until I thought I was going to choke - on the very thing I was trying to breathe.

To make matters worse, at that very moment a lump of coal fell inwards, down into the glowing heart of the fire, sending up a shower of sparks. A puff of dirty black smoke billowed outwards into the middle of the room, making my eyes smart and water, I coughed and retched.

Although my mind was in turmoil, of one thing I was now certain. Something I think I'd known all along, despite my feeble efforts to convince myself to the contrary. My recent experiences here in Hereford, at Marsh Leys Hall, at the inn, on the train, were in fact incapable of rational explanation, were somehow, ghostly.

Why I should have come to accept that now, and not before, I couldn't say. But although it was something I'd never experienced before in my life, once accepted, I was in no doubt about it, none at all.

"What *is* it? What do you want of *me*? You asked for my help? How can *I* help you? What can *I* do? *Why me*?" I whispered.

But why me indeed? A lawyer. After all, my legal training scarcely qualified me to deal with the situation I found myself in now.

Indeed, by its very nature, my profession had taught me to deal in cold hard facts. Failing that, to seek to establish things evidentially - either on the balance of probabilities or beyond reasonable doubt. But how could I seek to apply the civil, let alone the criminal standard of proof, to something as intangible, as unearthly, as the supernatural?

To whom could I turn to for help? If it had been a legal problem, there were various journals, periodicals, statutes, precedents, here in my chambers, from which I could seek advice and guidance.

If that didn't resolve the matter, then I could ask Ferguson, Matthews, or any one of my colleagues, saving Wickin of course, even Mr Chapman, who, provided

*Whistle . . .*

you'd exhausted all other avenues of enquiry first, was only too willing to give of both his time and experience.

But this was different.

In any event, I'd spent several years studying hard to pass my law exams, and after that I'd had to work even harder, before being lucky enough to obtain my present position with Evans, Chapman and Jenkins, the oldest and most respected firm of solicitors here in Hereford.

I knew full well there would be no shortage of applicants for my present position, were I to be called upon to resign - on the grounds of what, no doubt, would euphemistically be termed, ill health. I wasn't about to risk throwing away all that I'd achieved here in Hereford over the last three years. No, this was something I had to sort out on my own.

Then there was Claire to consider. Despite the fact that we were to be married the following year, I didn't feel I could burden her with this.

In fact I think she sensed something had happened, that night we had supper together at the Green Dragon Hotel - if not before. I'd tried my best to make the usual kind of small talk, rather unsuccessfully as it turned out, and there were several awkward silences during the meal.

At one point, Claire even asked me if I was having second thoughts about our getting married. I said of course not, but I wonder if she believed me. Fortunately she didn't press me any further, and let the matter drop. Otherwise I don't know what I might have told her.

Yet I knew I couldn't stay here in my room. I knew that this matter, whatever it was, wherever it led me, whatever it cost me, had to be resolved. For reasons I did not yet, indeed might never, understand, I was the only person capable of solving it.

After all, if it hadn't been for my cursed curiosity in the first place, none of this would have happened. Or would it? Even if I'd carried on walking, gone straight back to the inn, not stopped to look round the hall, some sixth sense, hitherto dormant, deep within my innermost being, told me this, whatever it was, would have befallen me anyway, sooner or later.

Not that I believed in predestination. Or rather I hadn't, at least, not until today. But then, during these last few days, I'd been forced to come to terms with the fact that things I would once have dismissed as fanciful nonsense, and which had I been asked about before today, I would have said did not, could not, possibly exist - except within the pages of cheap fiction, in fact could and did exist. Were real, very real.

*. . . and I'll be there*

Because, whatever anyone else might think, indeed however much I might wish it otherwise, I could not deny the evidence of my own senses.

I had to know what lay behind this. I had to find out. More than anything, I desperately needed to know why.

Somewhat groggily I rose to my feet, and groped my way across the room. Somehow I managed to struggle into my outer clothes, opened the door, and made my way, rather unsteadily, along the passage.

Fortunately, when I reached the outer lobby, I found it empty. At that moment, the last person I wanted to see was Wickin. No doubt he was still detained in the Wig and Pen with his orders for luncheon.

Halfway down the wooden staircase, I met Ferguson coming up. We exchanged greetings.

"Are you alright Harris? You look dreadful."

"Thanks, Ferguson. You always know how to make a chap feel better."

"Sorry. I only asked."

"No, as it happens I'm not alright. I've got a lousy headache, and I feel all hot and shivery. Probably a touch of 'flu. I'm on my way back to my lodgings now. Have a hot bath, then straight to bed. I probably won't be in tomorrow, maybe not for the rest of the week. Would you let Mr Chapman know?"

"Of course," he smiled. "When I see him that is," he added. I must have looked surprised. "He's been closeted with the Dean over the way all the morning". Ferguson nodded his head in the direction of the Deanery. "Have you any appointments booked for this afternoon?"

"No, fortunately I haven't. If you remember, I was supposed to be in court until the end of the week. But old Whitey's gone down with influenza himself."

"Mind how you go."

"Thanks, I will."

I carried on down the staircase. When I reached the bottom step, I stopped and stood still. "Well, what now?" I thought.

I made my way outside and down the passage leading to Church Street, narrowly avoiding Wickin on his way back from his daily errand to the Wig and Pen. Crossing the Close, I headed up Broad Street towards All Saints' Church.

On the opposite side of the road, just outside the Green Dragon Hotel, a line of hansom cabs was drawn up waiting for fares, the horses mired up to their fetlocks in the deep slush of melting snow, their drivers warmly muffled against the cold, perched atop the rear of their vehicles.

Scarcely knowing what I was doing, I found myself stumbling across the

*Whistle . . .*

snow bound, rutted street, dodging the passing traffic, and hailing the nearest cab.

"Cabby! Oakfield House, if you please." The voice was mine, but the words were not; they seemed to come from someone else.

Opening the door, I climbed in, and settled myself back against the cold damp musty smelling leather of the cab. A moment or two later, I heard the driver call "Walk on" to the horse, and we were off, heading through the bustling snow covered streets, bound for the north side of the city.

For most of that journey, I paid scant attention to what passed beyond the misted windows of the cab. Instead I sat lost in thought. As we clattered past the United Counties Bank on the corner of Broad Street, then up High Town, and along Widemarsh Street, I told myself this was ridiculous. What was I doing, sitting here in this cab, bouncing along the road? What did I hope to find at Oakfield House? Indeed what could I possibly expect find, except another empty house?

Several times, as we bowled along the road, past the Post Office and Barrs Court station, I was on the point of banging on the cab roof with my gloved fist and telling the driver to turn round. But each time something prevented me from doing so. "Alright then", I thought, "you asked for my help. I'm here, now, it's up to you". I took a deep breath, clasped my hands behind my head, and closed my eyes.

I must have dozed off, because the next thing I recall was hearing the long grind of the cab wheel as it rasped against the kerb. A moment or two later and the driver opened the door.

"We're 'ere, sir, Oakfield House. That's what you wanted, wasn't it sir?"

"Yes, cabby. Oakfield House."

I clambered out of the cab and paid my fare. The cabby thanked me, touched his cap, and climbed back up onto his seat. A moment later and he was off, clattering down the road, leaving me alone on the deserted pavement outside Oakfield House.

For the second time that day, I found myself asking "What now?"

I thought I'd find another empty house, and so it seemed I had. Oakfield House stood alone in its own grounds. I thought the house looked somewhat austere and rather forbidding, set against the gathering sky of the winter's afternoon. No smoke issued from the chimneys. In fact, the property had a distinctly shabby appearance. An air of neglect seemed to pervade the whole place.

For a moment or two, I simply stood at the gates and looked up at the house.

*. . . and I'll be there*

It lay back from the road, separated from it by a long sloping lawn, bordered by a high brick wall pierced by tall wrought iron gates, set between two stone piers. A winding gravelled drive led up from the gates to the front door.

I could see the stucco rendering on the front of the house was both cracked and stained, the paintwork peeling. The windows of the rooms on either side of the front door were shuttered fast from within. Upstairs, someone had drawn down the blinds, now bleached as pale as bone by their constant exposure to the sun.

Despite the thick blanket of snow, the grounds also wore an air of neglect. Clearly, they hadn't been tended for some considerable time. Away to my left were the remains of a wooden summerhouse, now deeply shrouded in snow. In the middle of the lawn stood a large oak tree. Someone had fixed a swing to one of the lower branches. One of the ropes had broken. The seat hung down, trailing in the snow.

The whole place looked deserted, yet, oddly enough, I had the distinct impression that someone was watching me from somewhere within the silent, shuttered house.

I found myself pushing open the rusty iron gates and threading my way up the winding drive. Reaching the house, I walked into the porch and pulled hard on the bell by the front door. I wondered if it still worked. To my surprise, I found it did, as from somewhere, deep within the darkened house, came the faint, but unmistakable, ringing of a bell.

I stood waiting in the porch for quite some time for someone to answer the door, but no-one appeared. In fact, I think I'd have been rather surprised if someone had. Undeterred, I pulled on the bell again, and for the second time I heard it echoing through the empty silent house.

Undaunted, I rubbed the frosted glass of the front door, and peered inside. Dimly I made out the foot of a darkened staircase, and beyond it a narrow tiled hall, it was not much more than a passage, which ran backwards towards the rear of the house. Faintly, through the fanlight above the door at the far end of the hall, flickered the warm glow of lamplight. So I'd been wrong, there was someone here after all. Perhaps a caretaker, living in the servants' quarters, which presumably lay at the rear of the house.

I turned and made my way out of the porch. If Christopher and his mother were still living here, although I had to admit it looked unlikely, then of course there had to be another entrance, for tradesmen and for the servants.

I wondered if perhaps both Christopher and his mother had gone to spend Christmas with the boy's grandfather, old Sir James, at Lower Moreton Court.

*Whistle . . .*

Although, on reflection, that too seemed unlikely. In which case, whoever had been left behind to see to the house might well not bother to answer the front door. Of course such conduct wouldn't have been tolerated before the War, but then so many things had changed, and most of them not for the better.

It couldn't have been much after one o'clock, but already the sky had begun to cloud over. I turned to my right and made my way through the snow, round to the rear of the house.

Away to my left, beyond the remains of the summerhouse, I saw a small wooden gate set in the boundary wall. Footprints led from it, across the silent, snow shrouded grounds, towards the rear of the house. I turned the corner and found myself standing in a large open space, one side of which was closed off by a wing projecting back from the house, which together with the rear wall of the main house formed two sides of a large courtyard. Facing it was a range of dilapidated outbuildings, while on the fourth side of the yard stood a derelict coach-house and stableblock, flanking a stone archway, the double gates of which were both firmly shut and barred.

Lamplight glowed through one of the ground floor windows of what I took to be the servants' wing. Carefully I edged my way across the snow bound yard and knocked on the door by the lighted window. Inside the room suddenly went dark. A chair scraped back on the floor. Then silence.

I knocked on the door again and still no response. I went and stood by the window next to the door, rubbed the grimy glass with my gloved hand, and peered in.

"Hallo? Is there someone there? Perhaps you can help me? I'm a local solicitor and I'm making enquiries about someone I believe used to live here ... during the War."

Time passed whilst I stood my ground and waited.

I heard the sound of a bolt being drawn. Then, cautiously the door opened a few inches.

"Monsieur, can I help you?" said a woman's voice in strongly accented English.

My heart skipped a beat as I turned. In the half open doorway, eyeing me suspiciously from round the edge of the door, stood a young, dark haired woman, with penetrating deep set eyes. I judged her to be about thirty, possibly slightly younger, it was difficult to tell.

I recognised her at once of course, it was the young woman in the photographs.

"You must forgive my English m'sieur, even now it is not that good."

*. . . and I'll be there*

I raised my hat.

"Vous êtes française?"

"Mais oui. Parlez-vous français m'sieur?" She smiled at me, revealing a display of startlingly white teeth.

"Some," I said, "my grandmother came from near St Malo."

"How can I help you m'sieur?" the woman asked mildly.

"Forgive the intrusion, but I don't even know that you can. In fact I don't even know your name."

"Mathilde Moncontour, m'sieur. Et vous, vous êtes?"

"My name is Stephen Harris. As I said, I'm a solic ... a lawyer, here in Hereford. I am making some enq ... seeking some information about someone I believe ... used to live here."

"Who, m'sieur?" she said tersely.

"A Captain Maitland?"

The woman made a small sound. Her body stiffened and she whitened visibly. I heard her sharp intake of breath as she clutched the door tightly.

"Vous venez de son père, n'est pas?", she gasped, staring at me open-mouthed.

"Sir James Maitland?"

"Oui, bien sûr?"

"Why ever should you think that?"

"J'ai de bonnes raisons de le croire m'sieur," she said curtly.

"Well, whatever your reasons madame, most assuredly, I'm not from anyone, least of all Captain Maitland's father."

The woman stood looking at me thoughtfully for a moment, as if she was making up her mind about something. I found her dark eyes disconcertingly direct. Then slowly she nodded.

"Oui, m'sieur, I believe you," she said softly.

By now she had emerged from behind the safety of the door and was standing on the step. Suddenly she rubbed her arms vigorously with her hands, apparently conscious of the cold, and glanced up at the sky. I followed her gaze. Although the day had started promisingly enough, it had clouded over. Above our heads, the first few flakes of a fresh fall of snow, began to drift downwards out of the grey sky.

"Il fait froid m'sieur," and turning her head, she indicated the open doorway behind her with her hand. "Vous voulez entrer?"

"Merci, peut-être nous aurons beaucoup de la neige encore?"

"Peut-être," she said simply.

*Whistle* . . .

The woman stood to one side of the doorway. Taking off my hat, I stepped inside. Beyond the door lay a narrow stone flagged passage. In front of me, slightly to my left, stood another open door. I walked through it and found myself in a small cosy kitchen, with a quarry tile floor.

While the woman shut and bolted the outside door, I stood just inside the doorway and looked about me. A scrubbed deal table occupied most of the centre of the room. Apparently she had been darning a pillowcase when I rang the door bell. Along with needle and thread, it lay discarded, next to the oil lamp on the table. At the far end of the room, underneath an arched recess, flanked by two tall wall cupboards, stood a small cast iron range.

The woman followed me into the room. She closed the door and drew across it the heavy curtain which hung behind. Then she motioned me towards the Windsor chair which stood in front of the range.

I put my hat on the table, and went and sat down on the chair. Directly opposite me, a small window looked out onto what must once have been the kitchen garden. Outside the sky had darkened considerably, and it had begun to snow heavily. Leaning over the table, the woman turned up the lamp.

"Voulez-vous quelque chose à boire m'sieur?"

I nodded.

"Merci."

She fetched cups and saucers from off the small dresser which stood by the door leading to the outer passage, and placed them on the table.

Slowly I glanced round the room. Above my head, flanked by several photographs, one of which I thought I recognised, and two china dogs, a clock ticked steadily on the mantelpiece. Beneath the table lay a faded rag rug. A sewing machine stood underneath the window. Next to me a pan of vegetables simmered gently on the range. At my feet a black cat dozed contentedly in front of the fender. Outside the snow continued to fall and crystals of ice slid down the window panes.

Picking up a battered old kettle, the woman poured boiling water into a large blue enamel coffee pot. That done, she put the kettle back on the range, and set the coffee pot down on the table.

"It will be ready soon, m'sieur."

"Thankyou."

"De rien, m'sieur."

Leaving the coffee to brew for a while, she drew up a chair on the other side of the range and sat down facing me, with her back to the window.

"Donc, vous étiez un ami de Capitaine Maitland, m'sieur?"

*. . . and I'll be there*

"A friend, no, but I know of him," I said evenly.

"Yet I do not think I have seen you here before," she said coolly.

"As I told you, I'm a solicitor, a lawyer, here in Hereford. My chamb ... my firm acted for Captain Maitland in the past. There are certain matters which need to be resolv ... sorted out, put in order. This house for instance ..."

"Edou ... Capitaine Maitland told me I might stay here as long as I wished", she said indignantly. "Qui êtes vous...?"

"You knew Captain Maitland well?" I interposed quickly.

"Bien sûr," she paused, then bit her lip. "We were to have been married."

She fell silent for a moment. Her eyes filled with tears and I waited while she composed herself.

"I met Edouard in France, m'sieur ... à Paris."

"In Montmartre?"

"Oui, m'sieur, but how do you know of this?"

"I've see ... there are some letters, written by you, to Edward, several years ago. Captain Maitland kept them and they were in a strong box along with some other papers, some photographs, the lease on this house ... He left them with my firm for safe keeping, just in case he ..."

"De peur de ne pas retourner de la Guerre," she concluded softly.

"Did Captain Maitland's family know about his ... relationship with you?" I asked gently.

"They knew, but his father, he would not accept it. Jamais."

"Why ever not?"

"He did not think me good enough for his son."

"I see. Forgive me asking, but was that why Captain Maitland went out to Canada?"

"Mais vraiment."

"To Quebec?"

"Oui. To stay with Henri, my uncle as I was ... unwell m'sieur."

I paused.

"And ... your son madame. Christopher? Was he born in Quebec?"

"D'accord. You seem very well ... informed m'sieur", she said mockingly, but without any malice.

"And later, you returned to England?"

"Oui. It was Edouard's wish his son should go to the school he went to as a boy. A Win...ches...ter," she said the name slowly.

"I see...", I said.

*Whistle...*

"Edouard wished also to serve his country m'sieur, and I returned to stay with my uncle. Mais Christophe, il n'a pas aimé son école nouvelle. Sa famille lui manquait, m'sieur. He was ... ?"

"Homesick," I said.

"Oui c'est ça. I wrote many times to Edouard, and begged him to let me come here, to England. At first he would hear nothing of it. Bien sûr, he wanted the same education for his own son. It was the only time m'sieur, nous nous sommes disputés," she frowned.

"The only time you quarrelled?" I added.

"Vraiment. Perhaps not the only time, m'sieur." She smiled.

"But eventually Captain Maitland, he agreed?" I asked.

"Oui, enfin, Edouard agreed that Christopher should go to school here, à Hereford."

"At the Cathedral School?"

"Bien sûr. Edouard went there as a boy, before he was sent away."

"To Winchester?"

"Vraiment. I was to come ... to England. Edouard was on his way home, from India. We were to meet, à Winchester."

"And bring Christopher back here?"

"Bien sûr. A Hereford, Edouard, il avait loué cette maison."

I nodded.

"Yes, I know about the lease," I said.

"But when I reached Winchester, il y avait une lettre - d'Edouard. His regiment had been ordered to France. He could not see me so I brought Christopher here, on my own, m'sieur."

"I see."

"Enfin, just before Christmas, Edouard came home, to England. It was the first time Christopher had seen his father, for any time, since the War began."

"And after that, Captain Maitland returned to France?"

"Oui m'sieur. Edouard promised me, after the War, it would be different. We would be married and then he would take us ... to meet his father. You see, until last month, he knew nothing of his grandson."

"Until last month madame?"

"Oui. When I found out ... that Edouard had been killed, I wrote to his father."

The woman fell silent and a tear rolled slowly down her cheek. She brushed it away impatiently with the back of her hand.

"You wrote to Sir James Maitland? You told him ... about Christopher?", I

*. . . and I'll be there*

said, somewhat aghast. For what little I knew of Sir James Maitland did not lead me to believe that such a letter would meet with a favourable response. The woman's next words confirmed my fears.

"Oui, but he did not even answer my letter," she said sadly.

"Perhaps he didn't receive it?", I suggested.

"Peut-être m'sieur. I do not know."

"Do you have a photograph of Christopher?", I asked.

"D'accord."

At that the woman brightened visibly, then she smiled and rose to her feet. She took down one of the framed photographs from off the mantelpiece, and set it on the table in front of me.

"Christopher, m'sieur. Il est beau n'est pas?"

She poured out two cups of coffee.

"M'sieur."

"Merci."

For a moment I didn't answer her, but sat sipping my coffee, staring in amazement at the photograph she had placed in front of me. The coffee was both black and bitter, and scalding hot. Of course I'd expected to recognise Christopher instantly. After all I had already seen a photograph of him, now lying at the bottom of the metal dispatch box back at my chambers.

The photograph was of a young boy, his dark hair neatly parted, dressed in a white shirt with a falling lace collar, short black jacket and knickerbocker trousers.

But I was wrong.

I picked up the photograph and studied it intently for several minutes, then set it back down on the table. For the boy staring back at me from the photograph was a total stranger. I'd never seen him before.

"And Christopher? He's in Hereford, at the Cathedral School?"

"Non, m'sieur. You do not know? I thought you must."

"Know what?"

"Christopher. Il a disparu."

I put down my cup and looked at her in utter astonishment. For a moment neither of us spoke, and in the silence which followed, I suddenly recalled what Wickin had told me, about the disappearance of a boy from the Cathedral School.

"Christopher. *He's* the missing boy? The one from the Cathedral School?"

"Oui m'sieur. The police, they are searching for him."

"And I'm certain the police will find him, after all, young boys don't just vanish."

*Whistle . . .*

"But it is nearly a week m'sieur, and still they have not found him."

A sudden thought occurred to me.

"The soldier madame, the one who was apparently seen talking to Christopher?"

"Oui, m'sieur?"

"Do you think he might have known him? A friend of his father's perhaps?"

"Peut-être m'sieur. During the last year of the War, when Edouard came home, sometimes he brought other officers with him, from his own regiment. Christopher, he liked to talk with them."

"Do you remember anyone in particular?"

"Non m'sieur. Sauf il y avait un jeune soldat ... Je ne sais pas son nom, but like Edouard, he may even now be dead."

"One of the soldiers ... who stayed here madame?"

"Oui m'sieur. Christopher liked him, he was very young I think. Il était ... le serviteur d'Edouard."

"His orderly?"

"Oui exactement m'sieur. Edouard had known him, I think, since he was a little boy. Après tout il a trouvé le petit médaille ..."

"What medal madame?", I interrupted brusquely.

For one brief instant, the chill of the secret cold crept into the warm room.

She looked at me, somewhat startled.

"Not a medal, m'sieur, a little... How do you say? A ... badge. The one Edouard gave to Christopher. At Christmas. The young soldier, before he left, to see his grandmother, he told Christopher how he had found it."

"Was there anything written on the back of it?"

"Oui, an inscription, but how do you know of ..?"

"Do you recall what it was madame ? I must know."

"Mais bien sûr m'sieur." She regarded me fixedly for a moment, then said,

"A
Christopher
De son Papa
E.J.M.
1917

"Pourquoi m'sieur?"

"De rien madame, de rien."

*. . . and I'll be there*

She looked at me thoughtfully. A word of explanation seemed necessary.

"Like you madame, I too have my reasons", I said simply.

For a moment I sat silent, lost in thought. At my feet, the black cat suddenly sat up, blinked its amber eyes, arched its back, stretched out its front paws, then curled up and resumed its place in front of the fender.

"You have spoke with M'sieur Whitton?" she asked.

"Madame. Whitton?"

"One of the masters, at the Cathedral School. Perhaps you might speak with him?"

"Yes, perhaps I should". Although, privately, I wondered what good it could possibly do.

Christopher's mother could tell me little more about her son's disappearance. I finished my coffee, thanked her, and made my farewells, promising to let her know the moment I found out anything which might give a clue as to Christopher's whereabouts.

The woman led me through the silent empty house and unlocked the front door. Outside it had stopped snowing. She stood on the doorstep and watched me go. At the gates I paused and turned to wave farewell, only to find that she had already closed the door.

*Whistle . . .*

# At the Cathedral School

At the end of the road, I hailed a passing cab on its way back into the city. About half an hour later I alighted from it in Broad Street, not far from the cathedral. I paid my fare, then headed across the Close in the direction of the Cathedral School. I debated whether I should seek an appointment with the Reverend Henson, the School Headmaster, but then decided against it.

Halfway across the Close, I ran into a group of boys playing about in the snow. I asked them where I might find Mr Whitton. Dr Whitton as it turned out. Several of the boys pointed me in the direction of an imposing Queen Anne House, which lay just off the cathedral Close, not far from St John's Street. I thanked them and walked on. Behind me the boys resumed their snowball fight.

"College House" proclaimed the brass plate on the wall by the front door. I walked up the steps and rang the bell. A shy, dark haired, young parlour maid answered the door and I asked if Dr Whitton was in, then ascertaining that he was, asked if I might see him.

The girl waited while I handed her my hat and coat.

"This way if you please sir," she said.

I followed her across the wooden panelled hall and up the main staircase. At the top of the stairs, she paused and knocked softly on the door on her left.

"Come," said a voice from within.

The girl opened the door and showed me into a book lined study, not unlike that of Mr Chapman's, the windows of which overlooked the cathedral Close. A warm fire crackled brightly in the grate.

"Beggin' your pardon, sir."

"Yes what is it Ruth?"

"There's a gentleman to see you sir."

The man behind the desk looked up, then rose to his feet and came round to meet me.

"Yes, thankyou that will be all Ruth."

"Yes sir."

The girl bobbed a perfunctory curtsey, and then hurriedly left the room.

"Augustus Whitton, housemaster". He was a tall, sparely built man, with craggy features. His slow measured tone and rich accent betrayed his Yorkshire origins, from near Haworth, as I found out later.

*. . . and I'll be there*

"Stephen Harris. I'm a solicitor, here in Hereford, with Evans, Chapman and Jenkins. My apologies for calling on you unannounced, Dr Whitton."

We shook hands.

"Evans, Chapman and Jenkins," mused Dr Whitton. "A most respected firm, I believe, on occasion, even this School has seen fit to retain the services of your chambers. Please, sit down."

Dr Whitton motioned me to the chair in front of his desk and resumed his own seat. Placing his elbows on the desk, resting his chin on his clasped hands, he leant forward.

"Now, how may I help you Mr Harris?"

Briefly I told Dr Whitton of my interest in the Maitland family. He sat and listened, and from time to time, nodded his head. I thought it wise not to go into too much detail. So I confined myself to generalities, merely explaining my involvement in the matter to be that of settling the boy's late father's estate.

As I suspected, Dr Whitton could add little to that which the boy's mother had already told me.

"He disappeared nearly a week ago," Dr Whitton glanced at the calendar on his desk. "In fact, exactly a week ago tomorrow afternoon. We had just had the first heavy fall of snow, the night before he vanished. You may remember?"

I shook my head.

"I was in London all last week and have only just returned."

"Yes," continued Dr Whitton clasping his hands behind his head. "And of course, boys will be boys, always have been, always will be."

"Indeed," I said, and smiled.

"Otherwise, things might not have turned out as they did. Ah well."

Dr Whitton sighed, smiled, sat back in his chair, and looked past me through the window in the direction of the cathedral Close. I half turned in my chair and followed his gaze. Outside in the Close, the group of boys I had encountered earlier were still larking about in the snow.

"You see," continued Dr Whitton, "when Maitland disappeared, he and some of the younger boys had been out playing in the snow, round the cathedral, although of course the Close is out of bounds to junior members of the School". As he finished speaking, the image of Wickin's miserable face flashed through my mind.

"I see," I said gravely.

"But from what I can gather, Maitland was getting a bit of a drubbing, got rather fed up with it, and took himself off, over to the north porch. Sometime after

*Whistle . . .*

that he was seen talking to the soldier. Hughes knows more about the incident than anyone."

"Hughes?"

"Yes Tobias Hughes, here at the School. He's in Maitland's own year. He was the only witness to what took place. In fact, if I'm not mistaken, he should be over in Old School House. It's fortunate you called here today Mr Harris, otherwise you'd have had to wait until next term to speak to him."

"I'm sorry, I don't understand."

"Of course not, how stupid of me. Let me explain. Hughes' elder brother is getting married, so the lad's going down early for Christmas, by the four thirty train this afternoon."

Dr Whitton picked up the little brass bell which stood on his desk, and shook it vigorously.

A moment or two later, the door opened, and a fair haired, anaemic looking, bespectacled boy nervously put his head round the corner.

"Ah, Jones. See if you can find Hughes. He's probably in the trunk room, over in Old School House. Tell him I want to see him in my study, over here, immediately."

The boy nodded, then disappeared. Bolted might have been a more apt word, like a frightened rabbit.

"I usually take tea about this time of an afternoon. Would you care to join me while we wait?" Dr Whitton beamed at me and pointed to a pile of tea things laid out on a small table near the hearth.

It was only then, that I suddenly remembered I hadn't eaten anything since breakfast. "Shall we make ourselves a little more comfortable?" He indicated the two winged armchairs set either side of the fireplace.

"Thankyou, Dr Whitton. That would be very nice."

A short while later, after I'd eaten half a dozen or so cucumber sandwiches, not to mention most of the muffins, as we were drinking our tea, there came a light tap on the door.

"Come," said Dr Whitton.

A short, thickset, dark haired young boy entered the room. Closing the door quietly behind him, he came and stood by the housemaster's chair, casting a surreptitious sideways glance at me as he did so.

"You wanted to see me sir?"

"Ah, Hughes, yes. This gentleman is Mr Harris, a local solicitor. He is making ... certain enquiries." Dr Whitton paused and looked directly at the boy.

*... and I'll be there*

"Yes sir?"

"About Maitland ... Christopher Maitland," said Dr Whitton in his slow measured tone.

"I understand, Hughes, you were almost the last person to see Maitland, just before he disappeared?" I said.

The boy turned and faced me.

"Yes sir."

"Would you mind telling me about what happened that afternoon?"

"No sir, not at all, but there isn't really much to tell. We were mucking about in the snow ... here in the Close." Hughes eyed his housemaster cautiously. Dr Whitton nodded, and a faint smile flickered across his mouth.

"Yes, Hughes?"

The boy turned back to me.

"Well sir, Maitland was getting rather a pasting, being rolled around in the snow. Anyway, he told us to get off him. We didn't think he was serious, but when we didn't take any notice, he got rather angry. When we saw he meant it, we let him alone. He went off and sat down in the porch, the one over there." Hughes pointed through the window towards the north porch of the cathedral.

"I see, then what?"

"Well, we carried on messing about in the snow. Then, just as the clock struck four, I happened to look up and I saw this man. He was standing inside the porch, talking to Maitland."

"Can you describe him?"

"He was in uniform sir."

"A soldier then. Do you know which regiment ?"

"No sir, you see, I didn't really get a good enough look at him. Besides, it was already getting dark. Anyway, when I saw him talking to Maitland, I got up and wandered over".

The boy paused, I nodded.

"Anyway, I heard him telling Maitland he'd known his father, in the War I suppose. Then he said Maitland's grandfather was looking forward to seeing him ..."

"So he must have received the ..." I began.

"Mr Harris?" Dr Whitton was eyeing me from beneath his bushy grey brows.

"Oh, nothing, nothing at all. I'm sorry Hughes, you were saying?"

"Well sir, I didn't quite catch what he said next. You see sir, he spoke with a local accent."

*Whistle . . .*

"Who? The soldier?"

"Yes sir, he said something, about having to go to Marches first, before seeing John. None of it meant anything to me of course. But when he saw me, the soldier, he put his arm round Maitland's shoulders, and the two of them disappeared off into the cathedral. There was something odd about the way he walked."

"What do you mean?"

"The man sir, he had a limp", the boy looked nervously at me from beneath his dark thatch of hair.

"And Maitland? He didn't seem alarmed? Worried even?"

"No sir. In fact ... "

"Yes Hughes?", interrupted Dr Whitton.

"Well sir, as they went off, Maitland seemed really excited. He was looking forward to seeing John again. I heard him say so, I suppose he must have..."

"Must have what?", I asked.

"Maitland must have known him."

"Known who? The soldier?"

"No sir, his son, John."

"You made no mention of that to me Hughes, nor as I recall to the police," said Dr Whitton sternly.

"Well no sir ... "

"Why ever not boy?"

"Well sir, it didn't seem important," Dr Whitton grunted his disapproval.

"After all sir," added Hughes, somewhat hesitantly, "I wasn't sure." His voice trembled, he stood looking down at the carpet. The boy seemed to be almost on the verge of tears.

At which point, Dr Whitton intervened once again.

"As I'm sure you must be aware Mr Harris, during the last few days, the police have been making extensive enquiries both here in Hereford, and elsewhere, to try and trace both Maitland ... and the soldier. I regret to say, so far without success."

"Will that be all sir?", asked the boy.

"Yes, thankyou, Hughes."

Dr Whitton dismissed him with an imperious wave of his hand and Hughes made for the door. Just as he reached it, a sudden thought occurred to me, where it came from I couldn't say. I stood up.

"Wait just a minute young man."

"Sir?" The boy turned back towards me.

*. . . and I'll be there*

"You said the soldier mentioned about going somewhere?"

"Yes sir, Marches. Something like that." The boy was eyeing me warily, as if sensing further criticism.

"Do you think what you heard, might have been ... Marsh Leys?", I asked softly.

I was conscious of Dr Whitton watching me closely, almost as if he sensed I knew rather more about the affair than I was letting on.

"It could have been sir, but I can't really be sure".

Hughes cast a furtive glance at his housemaster.

"Will that be all sir?"

"Yes thankyou Hughes. Run along now boy," said Dr Whitton.

I nodded my thanks.

"Hope I've been of some help sir."

"Yes, thankyou, you have. Perhaps more than you know, and have a safe journey home." I smiled and the boy smiled back at me. Then he was gone.

"The name means something to you, Mr Harris?" asked Dr Whitton. "If so, perhaps you should inform the appropriate authorities", I resumed my seat.

"No, not really," I said, finishing my tea. "I just seem to recall reading it somewhere. That's all, nothing more. Anyway I'm probably mistaken, I'm awful at remembering names."

"Of course, until this matter arose, we were completely unaware that the boy was Sir James Maitland's grandson."

Smiling, I set down my empty teacup. "Indeed," I said.

Dr Whitton eyed me suspiciously for a moment. He seemed almost on the point of asking me something. Then his innate good manners prevailed, and he forebore asking me any further questions.

I stood up and held out my hand.

"Thankyou," I said, "you really have been most helpful."

Dr Whitton stood up and grasped my hand.

"If there is anything further. Should you need any assistance, anything at all..., then you know where I am."

"Indeed I do. You've been most kind and I'll see myself out. Thankyou once again Dr Whitton."

I stepped out into the raw chill and fading light of the December afternoon. Although the snow had kept off, a bitterly cold wind was blowing up from off the river, and already it was growing dark. Ahead of me the Close lay silent and deserted. The boys had disappeared.

*Whistle . . .*

Every so often the wind whipped up handfuls of snow from off the frozen pavement, driving them past me in a stinging spray of whirling flakes. On the far side of the Close, through the veil of driving snow, I caught sight of the lamp lighter beginning his evening rounds.

I hurried on, casting a cautious eye in the direction of the Deanery. I was anxious to get back to my lodgings as quickly as possible. After all, I had certain preparations to put in hand, and the last thing I needed now was to run into anyone from my chambers, least of all Mr Chapman.

Just as I passed the north porch of the cathedral, for one brief moment I thought I caught sight of someone sitting there in the gathering darkness next to the inner door. Probably just a trick of the light. That, or else a parishioner who'd arrived too early for Evensong. Above my head the cathedral clock struck four.

The rest of my journey home was uneventful. I made my way through the snow covered streets, across the bridge, and back to my lodgings in Wye Street.

Later that same evening, after an early but substantial supper, sitting in front of a roaring fire I hastily thumbed through my copy of Bradshaws. Then I penned a hurried letter to Claire, explaining I had to go away unexpectedly for a few days on business, but that I would be back by the end of the week, well in time for the concert on Christmas Eve.

That done, I banked down the fire in the sitting room and went into my bedroom, where I set about completing my preparations for the morrow. I must have gone to bed about midnight. I read for about half an hour, then I turned out the lamp. After all, I had an early start ahead of me in the morning.

Tomorrow I had a train to catch. Northwards, to Ludlow, and Marsh Leys Hall.

# The Sound of A Penny Whistle

The following morning, having posted off the letter to Claire, I caught the ten o'clock train from Barrs Court station, bound for Shrewsbury. This time I was not so lucky. The train was held up south of Leominster for nearly half an hour. Somehow a flock of sheep had managed to stray onto the line.

I'd intended trying to catch a glimpse of Lower Moreton Court as we passed through the station at Berrington and Eye. After all Mr Chapman had told me it was visible from the train, but in the end I missed seeing it. I must have fallen asleep.

Scarcely was the train under way again, or so it seemed, when it came to a complete standstill, this time at Woofferton Junction owing to the derailment of a parcels van. Whilst I was impatient to reach Ludlow, there was nothing I could do, except make the best of the situation while the gangers set to work and cleared the line.

When it became evident this was going to take some time, having already read and reread my newspaper, I opened the door of my compartment, jumped down onto the platform, made my way over the footbridge and marched off down the station drive for an early lunch in the refreshment rooms known locally, and I thought rather quaintly, as "Abraham's Bosom", on account of the local clergyman who patronised them.

After about half an hour or so, having finished lunch, I made my way back up to the station, to find that the line was almost clear. Even so, it was gone midday, when my train finally steamed into the station at Ludlow.

I was the only person to get off and, jumping down onto the platform, I slammed the carriage door shut behind me. The booking clerk punched my ticket and behind me a whistle blew. There was an answering toot from the engine, and the train puffed noisily out of the station, on its way northwards to Shrewsbury. Over in the yard there was much rattling and banging as a farm cart was loaded up with empty milk churns.

Retracing my steps of the previous Saturday, I made my way down to the end of the road leading to the station. I set off along Corve Street, looking for an inn where I might find a bed for the coming night.

This time, I hadn't bothered to wire ahead. The Unicorn was full, but, crossing over the road, I managed to engage a room at the Queens Arms, just by the bridge,

*Whistle . . .*

the only other inn in the street which looked passably tolerable. Telling the landlord I would be back about five, I left the Queens Arms, and walked briskly out of Ludlow.

I must have been about half a mile or so out of the town, making slow progress on account of the deeply rutted state of the road, keeping a eye out for the stile, when suddenly behind me, I heard the sound of hooves followed by the rumble of wheels.

I turned round and saw a loaded farm cart, lumbering slowly along the road from the town through the slush and the snow.

As it overtook me, I realised it was the same one I'd seen earlier that afternoon in the station yard. The driver slowed his horse to a walk and asked me where I was bound. I thought it wiser not to say too much, so I simply said I intended doing a spot of hill walking that afternoon, up above Downton. The driver, a local farmer, told me he'd heard there'd been a chap doing something similar just this last week.

"Really," I said, hoping I'd managed to convey just the right amount of surprise in my voice. The farmer was heading up towards Downton himself with a load of empty milk churns from the station. He'd have been almost home by now if the train hadn't been late. Been some trouble on the line, or so he'd heard.

"Yes, I know," I said, and told him what I knew of the morning's mishaps. I was welcome to a lift part of the way if I liked. "Thankyou very much", I said, and clambered up onto the seat next to him.

We chatted about this and that, as the cart rumbled slowly along the rutted surface of the road, passing through Bromfield where we crossed the stone bridge over the Teme, and then on along the Leintwardine road, our conversation punctuated by the rattle of empty milk churns.

"Are there many farms hereabouts?" I asked, if for no other reason than to make conversation.

Apparently not, at least not as many as there used to be. Labour was scarce for only a handful of those who'd fought in the War, and who'd been lucky enough to survive it, had wanted to go back to working on the land once the fighting was over. Several of the farms on the neighbouring estate were in a very poor shape. In fact one of them was derelict. The land had been rented out or sold off, and was being worked by the other farms in the neighbourhood, his own included.

"Which estate would that be then?", I asked innocently.

"Why, Maitland estate, of course. Sir James Maitland, miserable ol' bugger. 'im that owns Moreton Court, down Leominster way."

*. . . and I'll be there*

"Would the place you mentioned, I mean ..., the one you said was derelict..., be Marsh Leys Hall?"

"It would, but 'ow would tha be knowin' that then? Tha bist a furriner."

"A furriner?"

"Tha not bist from around these parts lad."

"Oh! No, I just seem to remember seeing the name on my map. It struck me as rather odd at the time."

The farmer seemed to accept my explanation.

"That not be all that be strange 'bout Marsh Leys lad, not by a long way, leastways not from what folk round 'ereabouts say."

For a moment I was silent. The man knew something, or did he? Probably nothing more than gossip and rumour.

"Well," I said at length, "I expect any old house attracts its fair share of stories, particularly if it's empty or isolated, and Marsh Leys is both, is it not?"

The farmer eyed me suspiciously. Whatever it was he knew, or had heard, about Marsh Leys Hall, he intended keeping to himself.

"Tha'd need ask Gilbert 'bout that."

"Gilbert?" I asked, the beat of my heart began to quicken.

"Arr! Gilbert Frewen. Lived at lodge, up at the Marsh Leys, afore the War. 'is muther still does. Leastways she did, last I 'eard, deaf as a post."

I persisted.

"And this chap, Gilbert?"

"'e's landed on 'is bloody feet that one 'e 'as and no mistake."

"Why's that?"

"'e's gorn and got 'imself job...as landlord, at inn, just 'cross Ludford Bridge. Rents place, off Walcot estate. From what I 'ear in town, Gilbert, 'e be talkin' 'bout buyin' place. Lawd knows with what. Afore the War, never 'ad two brass farthin's to call 'is own did Gilbert."

I felt the familiar cold finger of fear stab at the base of my spine. I shivered.

"Which inn would that be then?", I asked, trying to keep the pitch of my voice normal. Sensing what the answer might be, I gripped the edge of the wooden seat tightly with my hands.

"The Bell. Why lad, be yer needin' somewhere to lay yer 'ead tonight then?"

"No, I just wondered that's all," I said.

The cart rumbled on along the lane.

"Perhaps he's got some money put by," I said.

"Who? Gilbert? Lawd no lad, 'e always be a right bloody wastrel. Worked for

*Whistle . . .*

Maitland, 'e did, years ago, afore the War", continued the farmer. "So did 'is lads, Tom, just like 'is ol' mun. Bloody waster. Now Jack, 'e wur diff'rent, makings of a good farmer Jack 'ad. Daft bugger, went and got 'imself blown to bits in War. Only one of 'em with any real sense, 'part from Vera mind."

"Who's Vera?" I asked.

"Sister, 'ousekeeper up at the Court, leastways that's what she be callin' 'erself these days. Course sum folks round 'ere might say diff'rent. *Vinegar Vera*, that's what she wur called, when she wur a wench. Sour as a crab apple an' from what I be hearin', she hanna changed much. Whoa boy."

The farmer drew rein on the horse, and the cart came to a gentle halt by a field gate. This was as far as he could take me. As it happened, so engrossed had I been in what the farmer was saying, that it was not until he brought the lumbering cart to a halt, that I realised that I was still some half dozen or so miles from my destination. I thanked him and jumped down from off the seat into the snow. If, after all, I found myself needing somewhere to stay the night, I was welcome to spend it at his farm. It lay but a mile or so distant, over towards Leintwardine.

Then, having given me directions to his farm, and having told me to keep an eye on the weather as he thought it likely there would be more snow before nightfall, the farmer clicked the reins and set off down the track. I stood and watched him go, until both horse and cart disappeared from sight round a bend in the lane.

So as to get my bearings, I pulled a map out of my jacket, along with my compass, and studied it carefully. Having established the direction I should take, I stuffed them back into my pocket, climbed over the rickety wooden gate, startling a hare in the process, and struck off across the desolate fields towards the south-east.

As I made my way across the snow covered fields, my thoughts were concentrated on what I had found out. All of it, seemingly, just by chance.

Edward Maitland embarked on a relationship with a young French woman, Mathilde Montcontour. For whatever reason, Edward's father refused to countenance it. As a result of that, both Edward, and his mistress, had gone to live in Quebec, where, shortly afterwards Mathilde had given birth to a boy, whom they named Christopher.

The fact of the boy's birth had been kept secret from his grandfather until comparatively recently. Then, following Edward's tragic death on the Western Front, Mathilde Montcontour had written to the boy's paternal grandfather, presumably asking for assistance, financial or otherwise. Her appeal had, apparently, fallen on deaf ears.

*. . . and I'll be there*

Shortly after that Christopher, now aged twelve, had disappeared from his school in Hereford. If what Hughes had overheard in the porch of the cathedral, was what I thought it to be, then the disappearance of Christopher Maitland and Marsh Leys Hall were, indeed, inextricably linked.

After all, Marsh Leys Hall formed part of the Maitland estate. The house itself was both empty and derelict, and had been so for some considerable time. Although why I knew not.

But whatever the reason, stories had grown up about the house, they were common knowledge, both in and around Ludlow. The landlord of the inn where I'd stayed the night, who'd lived near Marsh Leys Hall when he worked for the Maitland estate, knew about them. So too did the farmer from Downton, he'd made that perfectly clear. Exactly what the stories were, I did not know but from my boyhood in Market Drayton, I could guess what form they might take. Perhaps it didn't matter, but somehow, this time, I knew it did.

Whether they had anything to do with the boy I'd seen near the hall, then later on the train, I didn't know that either, but once again, somehow I knew they did. How else could one explain the reaction of the landlord when I'd mentioned having seen the boy?

How did all of this relate to the disappearance of young Christopher Maitland? Other than the fact his family owned both Marsh Leys Hall and the land on which it stood, there was no obvious link. Yet there was one, of that I was certain.

Then there was Jack Frewen, the landlord's younger son, who'd been killed on the Western Front. Was it just possible that he and the young soldier, who'd been Edward Maitland's orderly, the lad of whom young Christopher had been so fond, were one and the same?

And if he was... The more I thought about it, although I had no proof, the more I became convinced that Frewen's father was somehow involved in young Maitland's disappearance. According to Hughes the man seen talking to Christopher walked with a limp. There must be many such men, soldiers newly returned from the trenches in Flanders.

As I scrambled over another gate, a sudden thought struck me. Hughes had said he overheard the soldier telling Christopher he would take the boy to meet his son, John. But there was no way Frewen could have taken the boy to meet his son, no way on this earth.

Because by then young Jack Frewen was already dead, blown to bits in the blood soaked mud of Flanders.

*Whistle . . .*

About an hour or so later, and still none the wiser, I found myself looking down on the smokeless brick chimneys of Marsh Leys Hall and I idly wondered how many years had passed since smoke had issued from those crumbling, derelict stacks.

I slipped and slithered my way down through the heavy snowdrifts and round to the front gate, where I stood still and looked about me.

The manor house, near where I'd seen the boy, and the derelict outbuildings, seemed more dilapidated than ever. The place was deserted. Away to my right, silent and dark, lay a dense patch of woodland, the bare black branches of the trees heavily shrouded in snow.

"Now what?", I thought.

The air was heavy and chill, everything was quiet. There was no birdsong, not even a breath of wind. The same eerie silence I'd felt before hung about the house. Yet despite that, if indeed not because of it, somehow the very air seemed charged with tension, as it had been at the inn. Almost like the lull before a storm, when even the birds fall silent.

I glanced up at the leaden December sky. The farmer had been right, there would be more snow before nightfall, and, unless I was much mistaken, plenty of it. Above me, the winter sun was already beginning to sink westwards.

Somewhere, inside the empty house, a door slammed shut. Instinctively I looked up, shivering, as a sudden chill brushed the surface of my skin. The chill of the secret cold, my blood felt as if it had turned to ice.

The boy was standing just in front of the porch, at almost precisely the same spot where I'd seen him that first time. I stared at him in utter disbelief, scarcely believing the evidence of my own eyes. How long I stood there, I have no idea. Then suddenly, the boy turned, and disappeared inside the porch.

In a moment, I was through the gate and running across the snow covered garden, along the path and up the steps, towards where the boy had been standing. In my haste, I tripped on a loose flagstone and went sprawling. Picking myself up, not even bothering to stop to dust off the snow, I ran on up to the house. Reaching the porch, I raced inside.

It was empty.

The boy was nowhere to be seen, it was almost as if he had never even existed. Ghostly or real, I knew I'd seen him, I tried the door but it refused to budge, it was shut fast.

My whole body was shaking and my mouth dry as I sat down heavily in the porch. My breath was coming in rapid painful gasps. Tears of despair and

*. . . and I'll be there*

frustration welled up in my eyes and spilled unchecked and unheeded down my cheeks. If only I hadn't tripped on that damned flagstone.

Outside, beyond the porch, it suddenly seemed to grow very dark. Rather unsteadily, I rose to my feet and ventured outside, only to find I couldn't see more than ten feet in front of me.

No more than five minutes had passed since I ran into the porch, but in that short space of time, everything, the garden shrouded in its mantle of snowy white, the derelict outbuildings, and beyond them the surrounding countryside, had disappeared from sight, hidden beneath a dense blanket of swirling fog which had risen up from off the frozen ground and blotted out the view.

I was trapped.

I had no alternative but to wait until the fog cleared so I turned and walked back into the porch. Ahead of me, beneath its cracked and sagging lintel, stood the heavy front door. More in desperation than anything else, I walked up to it and beat against the solid unyielding timbers with the palms of my hands until they hurt. To have come this far and for nothing. I turned away.

Just as I did so, I heard the faintest of sounds. Scarcely believing my ears, I turned round and walked the few steps back to the door. I took hold of the latch and pressed down firmly with my thumb. Nothing happened, the door refused to open. Then suddenly, just as I was contemplating whether or not to try my shoulder against it again, to my utter amazement, of its own accord the heavy wooden door suddenly swung silently open on its rusty hinges. Stooping down under the low archway, my whole body shaking, I stepped nervously inside Marsh Leys Hall.

From the very moment I set foot across the threshold, it became evident the house hadn't been lived in for years. Empty and forsaken, tenanted only by rumour.

In the entrance hall whole areas of plaster had fallen away from the ceiling, exposing the timber laths beneath. Ahead of me, in the darkness, something scuttled across the floor at the foot of the main staircase and disappeared through an open doorway. Probably a rat.

Silence descended once more.

I didn't dare go upstairs. The place was clearly dangerous, and I didn't think the floors above, let alone the staircase, would stand my weight. Instead, half fearful of what I might find, I wandered slowly through the empty, long abandoned ground floor rooms, meeting nothing but darkness and cold air. All of the rooms showed similar signs of decay and neglect, the grates empty, the walls bare, stained with damp and mildew, the floorboards rotten. It was difficult to be sure

*Whistle . . .*

what particular use they had once served, not that it really mattered. In one the wooden panelling had been stripped from the walls, exposing the bare stonework beneath.

The whole place stank of damp and dirt. The cold of the past couple of weeks seemed to have settled into the very stones of its crumbling walls. That apart, there was a distinct chill in the air, which grew deeper with every step I took. Somehow each room seemed colder than the last.

Eventually I found myself in the room I'd looked into from outside, the one with the quarry tile floor. It looked much as before, with its heavily beamed ceiling, the cast iron range, covered in rust and grime, but I had the strangest feeling that somehow, something was different.

I had it now, or so I thought. A heavy fall of soot from the chimney had spilled out onto the floor, carpeting the quarries in front of the range. My heart missed a beat as there in the soot at my feet was the unmistakeable imprint of a pair of boy's boots.

For a moment, I was too unnerved, even to move. I could feel the rapid pounding of my heart beating against the walls of my chest. In an attempt to steady my nerves, I clutched hold of the rusty iron range. If I hadn't done so, I think I might well have taken to my heels and run out of the house.

There was something else too, I felt sure of it. Without releasing my hold on the range, I let my eyes travel slowly round the room, from floor to ceiling and back again. Nothing different there. The window, its panes cracked and dirty, that hadn't altered. There were also the two doors, the one leading upstairs, and from where I was standing I could see the first two or three steps of the wooden staircase.

The other door leading down to ... that was it. The second of the two doors, the one with the steps leading down to the cellar. It had been open on my last visit, but now it was shut fast.

Summoning up all my reserves of will power, I let go of the range, walked over to the door, lifted up the latch, and pulled it open. Beyond the door a short flight of steep stone steps led downwards into the darkness.

Cautiously, my whole body trembling, I began to descend the cracked slippery steps. Halfway down, one of the treads thrust upwards, I edged round it. At the foot of the staircase was a low arched doorway. The door had long since disappeared. Ducking down, I walked through the empty doorway, and into the cellar.

Daylight filtered fitfully through two small iron gratings set in the wall above

*. . . and I'll be there*

my head. The bars of one of them had disappeared, eaten away with rust. There was no way in through there, except, perhaps, for a small boy.

I stood still and gradually my eyes became accustomed to the gloom, but even if they hadn't, I would still have recognised the room, with its low ceiling, the beams thickly festooned with cobwebs and dust. The room in my dream.

My heart began to thud and my breathing became quicker. I was possessed of the unshakeable certainty that everything I'd experienced in the last few days had been designed to get me into this very room.

It was then I saw the lamp. In the stone wall, opposite one of the gratings, was a small dark recess and in it stood a battered hurricane lamp. I reached forward and picked it up. Although rusty, it was full of oil so evidently someone had been here, and recently too.

Setting it down on the floor, I lifted up the globe, turned up the wick, took out a match from my pocket, struck it on the wall beside me, and lit the lamp.

I rose to my feet, holding the lamp aloft and I looked about me. Apart from a few empty sacks lying on the floor at the far end of the cellar, and a pile of broken timbers in one corner, the cellar was empty. Even of ghosts.

But I was wrong.

Beyond me in the darkness something stirred and the faintest of echoes ran round the stone walls of the cellar. I stood still and listened intently. Yes, there it was again, the same sound. Faint and indistinct, yet instantly recognisable. From my childhood, years ago, I'd heard it often then, though not recently, not for a very long time.

Hardly believing what I was hearing, my heart pounding in my chest, I edged my way cautiously across the uneven floor. The sound seemed to be coming from the furthest corner, from beneath the pile of timber. As I drew closer, there was no mistaking what it was. After all, I'd had one when I was a boy. It was the sound of someone playing a penny whistle.

Setting the lamp on the floor, quickly I knelt down, tore off my gloves and began clawing desperately with my bare hands at the pile of timber, throwing aside the splintered joists and smashed rafters, heedless of the noise I was making.

After about five minutes, soaking with sweat, my bare hands filthy and bleeding, I cleared away the last of the timber. Beneath it lay what looked like the mouth of an old well. For a moment I knelt there, gazing at it, my breath coming in rapid gasps. In the ensuing silence, I suddenly became aware that the whistling had ceased.

*Whistle . . .*

The stonework round the top was both loose and dangerous. It would take but one injudicious move to send it hurtling down into the inky blackness below me. Kneeling as close to the edge as I dared, slowly I lowered the lantern into the darkness. The lamp shook and swung in my hand, casting flickering shadows on the crumbling stone walls. About twenty feet or so below me the shaft was blocked, choked with earth and stones fallen from above.

For one brief instant, caught in the flickering gleam of the lantern, something showed white against the dark heap of earth at the bottom of the shaft. Then I heard a slight whimper. I swung the lantern round, over to where the sound had come from. Cautiously I leaned forward and at the bottom of the shaft, huddled against the side, lying on a pile of rubble, saw a young dark haired boy.

"Christopher?", I called softly.

At the sound of my voice, the boy shifted round in the confined space and looked upwards towards the light. He blinked his eyes and almost imperceptibly nodded his head, but he was clearly terrified.

"It's alright Christopher," I said, "I'm a friend. Can you stand?"

The boy nodded again and slowly he struggled to his feet. As he did so, the pile of rubble beneath his feet shifted.

"Careful lad," I called.

Setting the lantern down on the edge of the well, I lay full length on the floor of the cellar, and stretched my arms down into the darkness of the shaft.

"Here, reach up to me. Yes, that's it." I felt the boy grasp my hands. Grabbing hold of his wrists, I began slowly to pull him upwards towards me and it took a while. The boy was clearly exhausted and I was worried any sudden movement might bring about a further collapse of the sides of the shaft.

"Now use your feet. That's right," I said, as the boy neared the surface. "That's it lad, against the sides."

A few moments later, and Christopher was huddled against me on the floor of the cellar, coughing and retching. He was filthy dirty, covered in dust and grime. Placing his face against my shoulder, he sobbed convulsively.

"It's alright Christopher, it's over lad," I said, putting my arm round his shoulders.

"I knew you'd come," he said brokenly, "he said you would." It was the first words he had spoken and clearly delirious, the boy began to shiver.

"Here," I said, grabbing several sacks from off the floor of the cellar and wrapping them about his shoulders, "it's the best I can manage at the moment. Do you think you can walk, if not I'll have to carry you."

*. . . and I'll be there*

The boy nodded.

Very slowly, the boy stumbling across the uneven floor, we set off. The cellar steps took a little longer but we managed it eventually though. At the top of the steps Christopher had to rest, all but spent. Half carrying, half dragging him, I staggered back through the empty rooms towards the front door.

It stood open, just as I'd left it. We had all but reached the door, when suddenly, from outside, seemingly close at hand, came the sound of a shot. Shattering the silence, it echoed and re-echoed across the frozen landscape.

The boy slumped down in the porch by the door, completely exhausted. He was breathing heavily, "I'll get help," I said.

Outside, the fog was thicker than ever, blanketing the snow covered garden, swirling through the trees, so that they stood out like silent ghostly sentinels.

I thought the shot sounded as though it had come from the woods, away over to the left of the overgrown drive, although of course I couldn't be certain. Praying I was heading in the right direction I set off. Dense freezing fog swirled all about me and several times I sank almost to my knees in the heavy drifts of snow. But eventually, after what seemed like an eternity, I reached the gate.

So long as I could find whoever it was who'd fired that shot, gamekeeper, poacher, I didn't care which, then my task of getting the boy back to Ludlow would be that much easier. But my ordeal was not over yet. I stumbled on through the heavy snowdrifts which covered the drive, till at last I found myself by the edge of the wood.

Here the snow was less deep, the going easier, but in the fog, the trees took on unfamiliar and menacing shapes. Low hanging branches barred my path and at one point a shadow swept silently across my path. Momentarily startled, I struck out blindly. The owl soared away from me, unperturbed, intent on seeking its own prey.

Catching my right foot in an exposed root, I clutched at the tree beside me, just in time to save myself from falling headlong into the snow, but not from a wrenched ankle. Regaining my balance, I stumbled on with pain striking through my ankle.

After about half a mile or so, the trees began to thin out and it seemed to be growing somewhat lighter. Ahead of me, a group of Scots pine loomed stark above the fog. As I drew closer, I could see there was something dark at the foot of the trees, lying among the frozen sea of bracken.

It was a man. Caught by his left leg, just above the knee, in a trap, the kind of which I thought had been outlawed years ago.

Judging by the depth of the snow, and by the amount of blood he'd lost, he must have been trapped for some time. The pain he was in must be well nigh

*Whistle . . .*

unbearable. His shoulders shook, his breathing was laboured and his breath coming in ragged gasps. A shotgun lay several feet away from him in the snow, fired, I assumed, in desperation, to try and attract someone's attention.

As I drew level with him, a look of relief flooded across the man's face.

"Oh mun. For Gawd sake, get me owt of 'ere," yelled the man. He didn't remember me of course, after all, why should he? But I knew him, it was the landlord of the Bell Inn, Gilbert Frewen.

I was certain of one thing, and because of that, my immediate response to him was indirect.

"And give me one good reason why I should?"

"Eh, mun, what's that yer say?"

"You know what I'm talking about. You kidnapped him didn't you? The Maitland boy."

"What boy? Maitland? Dunno what yer talkin' abowt. Broke me wrist and all I 'ave. When I fell. Well, what yer waitin' for mun ? For Christ sakes get me owt of 'ere."

"Stop lying Frewen. You kidnapped the boy. If you hadn't, none of this would have happened", I said hoarsely.

Recognition was dawning on him now.

"'ere, 'ow do yer know my name? I know yer, don't I? Yer were at the inn". He winced, nursing his broken wrist.

"What did you expect to achieve? Blackmail was it, for his safe return?"

"No," Frewen's eyes narrowed. He grimaced and blood welled between his fingers.

"What then?" I demanded savagely, grabbing him by the chin and jerking it upwards.

"An eye for an eye."

"What do you mean?"

"Nowt to do with yer, 'sides the old man. Be glad to see the boy dead, 'e would."

"Who would?"

"Who d'yer bloody think?", screamed Frewen, "Maitland. Now for Christ sake get me owt of 'ere."

"Sir James Maitland? The boy's own grandfather? I don't believe you, you're lying", I said incredulously. I let go of his head and for one brief moment I forgot my wrenched ankle, and set my weight on it. Pain spiralled upwards.

"Well yer better bloody well believe it", yelled Frewen, his face contorted by both pain and anger, "cos it's the God's own truth. Don't look so mazed". He

*. . . and I'll be there*

hawked and spat contemptuously in the snow. "That's right, Sir James bloody Maitland", he sneered, "why 'e's no better than them that's banged up in 'ereford gaol, even if 'e is a bloody magistrate and owns 'alf the county. As God is my witness."

"But then He isn't, is He?", I said softly, consciously shifting my weight onto my other leg.

"Believe what yer bloody well like, 'e found owt, 'bout the boy. My sister, she told me, Maitland wouldn't be 'avin' 'is precious estate go to some French tart's bastard. Not 'im".

"And that justifies what you tried to do?"

Frewen seemed not to hear me. He was becoming increasingly delirious, speaking again now, in a low muttered tone, seemingly to himself.

"Dunno how, but 'e got out 'e did, little sod. Led me a right dance, 'im and that damn' whistle, right into this bloody trap. When I catch up with 'im ..."

That Frewen should seek to blame the boy for his own misfortune so infuriated me, that to begin with I didn't take in fully what he was saying. Grasping hold of his chin, I forced his head backwards. "No he didn't", I yelled, "How could he when he was..."

I broke off what I was saying, suddenly struck by a suspicion, so unbelievable, so incredible, that had it not been for my experiences of the past few days, I would have dismissed it out of hand as an aberrant thought. I let go of Frewen and he sagged limply against the root of the tree.

"I give yer me word mun, 'e's alright. It's the truth, I ain't 'armed the lad. For Christ sake mun, get me owt of 'ere, I'm near bleedin' to death".

"The truth and your word are as different as night and day", I said with contempt.

"I mean it mun, I'll tell yer where 'e is. The lad, 'e's alright".

"You'd better pray he is. As for where he is, you're too late. I've already found him so you're looking at spending a long time in prison, assuming of course you make it that far."

Frewen moaned.

"I'll see about getting you out of that when I get back with the boy, and just in case you get any ideas..."

I picked up the shotgun and flung it away from him. It landed with a soft thud in the snow. Stupid of me really for in my haste, I hadn't even checked to see if it was loaded.

"No, don't leave me mun, for Christ sake".

*Whistle...*

Ignoring Frewen's screams, I limped off back towards the drive. By the time I reached the house, Christopher had blacked out, weak from lack of food. I tried to revive him, by rubbing handfuls of snow across his face, but to no avail so I had no choice but to carry him. I hoisted him clumsily onto my back and my injured ankle screamed its protest. So much so, that I almost pitched forward into the snow.

Then a second shot rang out.

Relief flooded through me for it meant there must be someone else about. I staggered out into the snow, my hands numb with cold, the boy a dead weight on my shoulders.

I floundered through the heavy snow, down across the garden, along the drive, and into the wood. I began to shout, yelling myself hoarse to attract attention and I made for the grove of pine trees. If I was not mistaken, the second shot had come from the same direction as the first, and in that, at least, I was right.

Frewen lay slumped at the foot of the trees. The second shot had blown the back of his head clean off, and blood mixed with fragments of bone and brain lay spattered across the snow. Yet I'd thrown the shotgun well clear of his reach. So how on earth had he managed to get hold of it, let alone place it in his mouth, and pull the trigger?

There was no way Frewen could have done that.

Not with a broken wrist.

Not unless he'd had help.

But apart from Christopher and myself, there was no-one else about. Not another living soul, unless ... a shiver ran down my spine. No, that was impossible, or was it?

Shielding the boy's face against my coat, slowly I edged past the sprawled body, and set off for the drive. It took me some time to reach it, what with the weight of the boy on my back, and my injured ankle, but somehow, reach it eventually I did.

I must have stumbled along the drive for upwards of at least a mile. With every step I took, the pain in my ankle grew worse; the boy a leaden weight about my shoulders.

I reeled onwards, all but blinded by the snow, which had begun to fall heavily. My fingers were so numb I could hardly feel them, never had I felt so cold, so utterly exhausted.

I had all but expended every ounce of strength I possessed and my heart was beating wildly. I swayed from side to side like a drunkard and I could no longer

*. . . and I'll be there*

even trust to my own senses. I began to hear voices, and pinpricks of light danced before my eyes. Ahead of me, shadowy figures emerged out of the snowy darkness.

Somewhere, in the distance, I thought I could hear the furious ringing of a bell. The last thing to register in my brain, as overcome with cold and fatigue, I pitched forward into the snow, and into the blessed relief of unconsciousness.

Behind me the sky had turned an angry red.

Marsh Leys Hall was on fire.

*Whistle . . .*

# Christopher

The house was burnt to the ground. The fire engine from Ludlow tried to reach it, but couldn't get through on account of the heavy drifts of snow which had blocked the drive, and by the time the firemen had dug their way through, it was too late to save the house. All they could do was stand and watch it burn. I understand the fire made newspaper headlines right across the county.

When asked about it later, I couldn't remember whether or not I'd extinguished the lantern I'd lit in the cellar, and of course there was a great deal of wood lying about. I didn't say so at the time, but privately I thought most of it would have been far too damp to burn. So the exact cause of the fire which swept through Marsh Leys Hall that night remained a mystery. Of course I didn't find out about the fire, nor about what workmen engaged upon demolishing what little remained of the house had found at the bottom of the well, until some time later.

Apart from the physical injuries I had sustained as a consequence of that night in the snow, I suffered something close to a mental breakdown as a result of my experiences at Marsh Leys Hall. Indeed, I was very ill for several weeks.

After two days spent in a room at the cottage hospital in Ludlow, Claire's uncle, accompanied by his wife and Claire herself, collected me in his motor car and drove me back to Hereford. Despite my earlier promise to Claire, I missed the Christmas Eve concert in All Saints' Church after all!

The next few weeks I spent convalescing at Claire's parent's home. I needed light, warmth and people round about me, so Christmas, and the festive season, provided me with exactly the tonic I so desperately needed.

Claire's parents were kindness itself, neither they, nor Claire herself, asked anything of me. Nor did they press for any explanation as to what had happened, leaving me to decide if and when, I should choose to take them into my confidence.

Claire was with me every day and I spent most of my time, warmly wrapped, sitting in front of the fire in the drawing room, either dozing or reading, my meals brought to me on tray. To a certain extent the days merged into one another. I even managed to teach Claire the rudiments of chess. Gradually, the phantoms which haunted my sleeping hours dwindled, they faded and then were gone.

Early in the New Year I received a visitor. It was Mathilde Montcontour, from her I learned something of what had befallen young Christopher after he vanished from the Cathedral School.

*. . . and I'll be there*

Lured, unsuspectingly, onto the five o'clock train bound for Shrewsbury, then taken by pony and trap from the station at Ludlow to the lodge up at Marsh Leys Hall - all on the pretext of meeting not only Jack Frewen, but also Christopher's paternal grandfather - Sir James Maitland.

Frewen had managed to make it all sound very plausible, especially to an impressionable twelve year old boy still devastated by his father's death. Whilst Christopher should have perhaps been somewhat more circumspect, Frewen's undoubted knowledge of the Maitland family, coupled with the fact that he was young Jack's father, made what he said seem perfectly credible, and served to allay any suspicions the boy might otherwise have had.

Unfortunately his mother's decision to withhold certain details of exactly how his father had died, in order to soften the blow, had only served to heighten Christopher's natural curiosity. So when Frewen told the lad his own son Jack had been alongside Christopher's father when he was killed, it was only natural that Christopher would seize the opportunity thus presented to find out more about what had happened to his father.

Then, after he'd seen Jack, Frewen assured Christopher he would take him on to Lower Moreton Court to meet his grandfather. In fact, his mother was already there, awaiting his arrival. Which of course was why Frewen had been sent to fetch him, only of course, he hadn't.

Exactly when Christopher realized all was not as it seemed, remained unclear. Not that it really mattered, as by then it was already too late. For nearly a week he had been kept bound and gagged, fed, albeit meagrely, locked in the attic of the lodge, while Frewen decided what to do with him. When it came to it, Frewen found he didn't have quite the stomach he thought he had, at least not for the cold blooded murder of a frightened twelve year old boy.

Frewen's mother of course knew nothing of the boy's presence. She was over eighty, bedridden, and, as I recalled afterwards, stone deaf.

But having come this far, Frewen obviously couldn't let the lad go. Then, towards the end of the week, under the cover of darkness, Frewen had dragged the terrified boy through the snow, up to the house, and thrust him down the derelict well beneath the cellar floor of Marsh Leys Hall, intending that starvation would achieve that which he could not bring himself to do.

By the time I found him, Christopher had already spent nearly two days incarcerated at the bottom of that well shaft. What that boy must have gone through could scarcely be imagined, let alone the wickedness which had contrived it.

87

*Whistle . . .*

Mathilde left, promising to return, and that next time she would bring Christopher with her. A week or so later she made good her promise. Christopher was almost fully recovered from his ordeal. Indeed his progress on that score had been somewhat more rapid that my own and I must confess our meeting was somewhat emotional.

I took the opportunity thus afforded by his visit to return to him the little cap badge. I don't think Christopher ever expected to see it again. Naturally, he wanted to know how it had come into my possession, something I should have foreseen. So I said I understood one of his friends had found it in the cathedral Close, and handed it in at my chambers. It was the best explanation I could contrive, even for a lawyer - at least at short notice.

Then Christopher started to ask me if I knew which of his friends had found the badge but I shook my head. Fortunately, just at that moment, Claire entered the room to tell us that tea was ready, and quietly I let the matter drop.

Several days later, on a bright morning towards the end of January, while I was sitting musing by the fire, Claire jolted me out of my reverie by reading out Sir James Maitland's obituary from the Times newspaper. Apparently he had been all but bedridden for several years, and had succumbed to the bout of influenza then sweeping the country. But somehow, try as I might, I could not equate the fulsome eulogy which appeared in the newspaper with what little I knew of the man.

During my convalescence, I even received a visit from Mr Chapman and I found him surprisingly sympathetic. He imparted one minor matter of interest, which he thought I might find amusing. Wickin's letter to the solicitors in Leominster had been returned to our chambers. Messrs. Wynn, Williams and Wynn, it transpired, were a firm of corn chandlers and they were extremely mystified as to why we should have written to them in the first place.

Mr Chapman put it down to carelessness on Wickin's part. Despite protestations of innocence, not only was Wickin required to write an abject letter of apology for any inconvenience caused, but Mr Chapman had him hunting high and low for the original letter from Leominster. So far it had not come to light, indeed, it was almost as if it had never even existed. But any thoughts I had on the whereabouts or otherwise of the missing letter, I kept to myself.

Just before he left me, to conclude matters at the Deanery, Mr Chapman made it perfectly clear that I was only to return to work when I was fully recovered.

In due course I had to give a statement to the police. Suffice it to say I kept it as brief as I thought was consistent with the truth. The jury at the Coroner's Court,

*. . . and I'll be there*

held in Shrewsbury, duly returned a verdict of suicide on Gilbert Frewen, which given the apparent manner of his death was hardly surprising. I saw no reason to disagree with it, none whatsoever. After all there were certain things I felt best left unsaid.

Early in February, shortly before I returned to work, Claire and I spent a few days down at Tenterden in East Sussex, where she had relatives. Whilst there I told her most, though not all, of what had happened, ever since I had first laid eyes on Marsh Leys Hall.

On our return to Hereford I found a letter awaiting me at my lodgings in Wye Street, postmarked from Leominster. I must confess I was a little nervous as I opened it, but, as it turned out, there was no real cause for alarm.

It was from Sir James Maitland's daughter, Lady Rosalind Aubrey. She had but recently returned from India with her children, following the death of her father. She was, it transpired, most anxious to meet me.

Should I feel sufficiently recovered to make the journey to Lower Moreton Court, she would have me met off the afternoon train the following Saturday. However, if I was still indisposed, or the date was at all inconvenient, she would of course understand.

I wrote back advising that I would be glad to meet her. The date suggested was perfectly convenient and, after all, what else could I do?

The following Saturday Claire saw me off on the early afternoon train to Shrewsbury from Barrs Court station. Not I believe without some trepidation on her part. It was, after all, the first journey I'd undertaken on my own since my expedition to Ludlow, and Marsh Leys Hall.

But if Claire had any misgivings about what I was undertaking, she kept her fears to herself. She even offered to come with me, but made no protest when I said I felt this was one journey I should make on my own.

A short while later that same afternoon, I found myself stepping down on to the platform of the small wayside station of Berrington and Eye, just north of Leominster.

Outside in the station forecourt, a pony and trap stood waiting by the gate. A gawky, sandy haired, beanpole of a man lounged beside it. On seeing me, he straightened up, pushed his hair back from off his forehead, then walked towards me across the gravel. He was the first to speak.

"Mr 'arris, is it sir?"

I nodded. The man touched his cap.

"Ekeels, sir."

*Whistle . . .*

"Pardon?", I queried.

"Ekeels, sir." He repeated his name again. "From the 'ouse. I've bin sent to meet yer." There was something vaguely reptilian about him, what with his thin snakelike body and pale watery eyes, I thought the name suited him.

A moment or two later, once I had clambered aboard the trap and was seated next to Ekeels, with a thick blanket tucked about my legs and feet, we set off

"Is it far to the house?", I asked.

"'bout two mile, sir, to the park gates, and 'bout same ag'in". The man seemed disinclined to talk. Nor was I much in the mood for conversation myself, and after that brief exchange no further words passed between us. The trap ran on through a maze of narrow lanes, between high banks topped with low stunted hedges. Warmly wrapped against the chill of the February afternoon, I sat silent, lost in thought.

At length we reached a turning to the left leading to a pair of massive wrought iron gates, flanked by two stone built lodges. Smoke from one of the chimneys spiralled slowly up into the chill afternoon air. We bowled through the open gates and rumbled over a cattle grid.

Shortly after that, I caught my first sight of Lower Moreton Court. Beyond the lodge gates, bordered by a tall cast iron fence, lay an vast expanse of parkland, dotted with large numbers of trees. The gravel drive wound on across the park for several miles, eventually passing through the archway of a small gatehouse.

Through the trees I made out a walled garden. Away to my left, on the far side of a large lake, was a small boat-house, and beyond it a brief glimpse of the Black Mountains, some twenty five miles away towards the south west. The drive swung back on itself, and continued round to a large gravelled area laid out before the west side of the house.

In front of me stood a substantial, beautifully proportioned, three storey house, built of reddish sandstone under a low slate roof. A broad flight of shallow stone steps, flanked by a pair of elegant cast iron lanterns, led up to a tall entrance door, set under an ornate portico.

As the trap pulled up, three young boys, all of a similar age, hurtled round the corner of the house. I recognised one of them as Christopher. When he saw me, he called to the other two, and all three of them ran across the gravel to meet me.

"Hello, Mr Harris, these are my cousins..., Edmund and Roland." Rather self consciously, one after the other, the two young boys each held out their hands.

"Pleased to meet you sir."

"And I you."

*. . . and I'll be there*

"Have you come to see Aunt Rosalind?" This from Christopher.

"Indeed, I have." A word of explanation seemed in order. "We've some matters to discuss." I added, then wished I hadn't.

The boy eyed me cautiously, "About me?", he asked.

"I've no idea." I said amiably.

"Will I see you before you go?"

"Surely."

"Race you to the boat-house," shouted Christopher, and ran off across the lawns towards the lake, hotly pursued by his two cousins.

I turned back to the driver.

"Thankyou," I said. Ekeels touched his cap. Then, clicking the reins, neatly he turned the vehicle about, and drove off back down the drive, leaving me alone at the foot of the steps.

While I was watching him depart, the front door had opened. A short, sharp featured, dumpy woman, with greying hair, red-rimmed eyes, dressed entirely in black save for a white blouse, stood watching me from the doorway.

I walked briskly up the steps and raised my hat.

"Yes sir?"

"Good afternoon, my name is Harris, Lady Aubrey is expecting me."

As I gave my name, the woman's green eyes narrowed to the merest of slits, feverish with hate. I all but found myself taking a step backwards.

"Indeed, this way if you please sir." She stood to one side of the door and indicated the stone flagged entrance hall beyond her. "I trust you had a pleasant journey... from Hereford ... Mr Harris?" Her tone was cold and formal.

I stepped inside. She closed the heavy door firmly behind me, all but plunging the dimly lit entrance hall into darkness.

"Your hat and coat sir, if you please."

I smiled and nodded. The woman stood waiting, tight lipped and I thought there was something vaguely familiar about her features, but in the dim light of the entrance hall I couldn't be certain.

"Thankyou, you're most kind."

"No need to thank me sir. I am merely carrying out my duties as housekeeper here," she paused. Then added, insolently, "however distasteful I may find them".

The woman was eyeing me now with a look, which verged almost on the impertinent. I stood her gaze, seeking to fathom her hostility. The reason for which suddenly dawned on me. The housekeeper, of course, then *she* must be Frewen's sister.

91

*Whistle . . .*

"Lady Aubrey is in the drawing room, I will inform her of your arrival. If you would be good enough to follow me sir," she said stiffly.

I followed her across the hall, and down a narrow passage, lined with hunting scenes. Save for the sound of my own footsteps, and the swish of the woman's long skirts on the floor ahead of me, the whole journey passed off in complete silence.

A short while later the housekeeper paused in front of a dark mahogany door.

"Wait here, if you please sir, and I will ascertain if Lady Aubrey is prepared to see you." That in itself was insulting for the woman knew perfectly well that Lady Aubrey had asked to see me.

"Of course," I said good humouredly, "you clearly know your duties." I paused and smiled at her, "But then a good servant always should." Dark patches of colour flamed across her cheeks and a muscle twitched involuntarily beneath her left eye. Evidently my parting shot had found its mark.

She knocked on the door, then went in, closing it firmly behind her. Beyond the door I heard the rise and fall of muffled voices. A moment or two later, and the door of the drawing room opened.

"Lady Aubrey will see you now sir," the housekeeper said curtly. She stood to one side and I walked briskly into the drawing room.

Seldom, I think, have I seen a more beautiful room. Panelled in wood, painted in white and gold, the walls lined with what I took to be family portraits, the furnishings exquisite, all set beneath an elaborately painted ceiling.

An elegantly attired woman, I judged her to be in her mid thirties, with honey coloured hair, sat by the marble fireplace. A bright log fire burned cheerfully in the steel grate.

Laying aside the piece of embroidery she was working on, and extending her hand, Lady Rosalind Aubrey rose to greet me. As I took her outstretched hand in mine, I caught the fragrance of her perfume. We shook hands.

"My dear Mr Harris, I am so delighted to make your acquaintance at long last and I trust you are now fully recovered from your ordeal?"

"Yes, thankyou," I said.

"Please, sit down." With a smile, she indicated a chair drawn up by the fire, opposite her own.

The housekeeper remained standing by the open door, her outwardly calm appearance betrayed only by the swift rise and fall of her chest.

"That will be all," said Lady Aubrey crisply.

"Ma'am." I heard the swish of the housekeeper's long skirts on the drawing room carpet.

*. . . and I'll be there*

"You are warm enough Mr Harris?"

"Yes, thankyou," I said somewhat distractedly, watching the door as it closed softly behind the housekeeper. I heard her footsteps echoing along the passage, then they faded out of earshot.

I looked up, to find Lady Aubrey eyeing me quizzically from beneath arched brows. Her eyes were cornflower blue.

"You seem not entirely at ease Mr Harris. Should I..."

I shook my head, not wishing to admit that I had found myself disconcerted by a mere servant, it took me a moment to find the right words to convey my feelings.

"An unpleasant woman," I said dryly, "nothing more."

"As it happens I entirely agree with you Mr Harris. Not that this household will be troubled by Mrs Mcghie's presence for very much longer, as yesterday afternoon I had occasion to go over the household accounts. There are ... certain ... irregularities... financial irregularities. Her employment here has been terminated, she leaves at the end of the week."

"Do you intend preferring charges?"

"As to that Mr Harris, I am still undecided, and perhaps after all there are worse sins..."

It was my turn to look quizzical and Lady Aubrey smiled.

"All in good time Mr Harris."

"But I am correct in assuming that your housekeeper is..., was Gilbert Frewen's sister?"

My hostess inclined her head and a faint smile etched the corners of her mouth.

"Did she know anything of her brother's plan to abduct your nephew from the Cathedral School?"

Lady Aubrey shook her head.

"Apparently not. I am given to understand that all she did was tell him where Christopher and his mother were living ... in Hereford. The authorities are satisfied she played no other part in the matter."

"Do you believe her?"

"In that, if nothing else."

She was silent for a moment.

"Now Mr Harris, would you care for some tea?"

"Thankyou, that would be very nice."

Reaching forward, Lady Aubrey pressed the bell push on the wall beside her. A few moments passed. There was a light knock at the door, and a small pasty

*Whistle . . .*

faced girl with mousy hair, dressed in black, with a crisply starched white apron, entered the room.

"Ah, Alison."

"Yes mum?"

"Alison, ask cook to prepare tea."

"Yes mum."

"For *two*, Alison." Lady Aubrey stressed the second word carefully.

"Yes mum, of course mum."

Colour washed over the girl's face. She bobbed a hurried curtsey and quickly left the room.

"Young girls these days." Lady Aubrey sighed as her eyes followed the girl's retreating form. "But now, to other, more important matters."

For a moment she sat back in her chair, fingering the delicately crafted cameo brooch at her throat. Then, seemingly having made up her mind about something, she placed both her hands gently in her lap and looked directly at me.

"I would like you to tell me your part in all of this, Mr Harris. Naturally I have spoken with Christopher's mother, and learnt of certain ... matters," she paused momentarily. "And yet ... even now, I have the distinct impression ... that the whole story has not been told."

I began to speak, but as Lady Aubrey held up her hand for silence, I paused. She nodded and smiled.

"Thankyou, no, unless I am very much mistaken, Mr Harris, not even to the authorities, and for that I thank you, but will you not at least, tell it to *me*?"

And so I did.

As I began to speak, her eyes came up and fastened on me. Lady Aubrey listened to me without interruption, her face impassive, her eyes never once leaving my own, except for when the maid brought in the tea. Briefly she put her forefinger to her lips and I waited while the girl set down the tray containing the tea things. Somewhere, outside the window, a blackbird began to sing, then, once the maid had gone, Lady Aubrey nodded, and I continued.

I left nothing out, beginning with my walk in the snow in the hills up above Ludlow, my strange experiences at Marsh Leys Hall, at the Bell, on the train, and in Hereford, my visit to Oakfield House and my meeting with Mathilde Moncontour, my enquiries at the Cathedral School, culminating in my return to Marsh Leys Hall, my finding Christopher, what Frewen had told me, and the manner of his death. By the time I had finished, the evening shadows had already begun to lengthen.

*. . . and I'll be there*

"The rest I believe you know already," I said.

This time, I thought the silence would never end. Beside us on the table the tea had gone cold and the sandwiches remained uneaten.

"Thankyou Mr Harris, I can imagine what it must have cost you to relive what you have suffered."

Through the drawing room windows came the sound of the three boys, still at play.

"And Christopher? He seems fully recovered?"

"He is. Of course at that age..." she smiled.

"They do well together."

Lady Aubrey rose from her seat and naturally I began to do likewise.

"Please, Mr Harris, remain seated, there is something I would like you to see."

She walked purposefully across the drawing room, towards a small table which stood in front of one of the windows. From where I was sitting I could see the top of it was cluttered with innumerable knick-knacks, small vases of flowers, pictures, photographs and the like.

A moment or two later, and she was once again seated in front of me.

"I would be grateful if you would look at this." In her hand was a photograph, mounted in a plain ebony frame which she held out to me.

"Take it, please."

I did as she asked, and as I did so, felt the hairs on the nape of my neck begin to rise, and although I was seated by the fire, for one brief moment an icy chill seemed to descend on the room. I had felt it before, the chill of the secret cold.

The photograph was of a young dark haired boy, smartly dressed in a school uniform, holding a boater. An exact copy of the one I'd found in the metal despatch box back at my chambers.

I was conscious of Lady Aubrey's eyes upon me. I raised my head and our eyes met. No words passed between us, there was no need. As I handed her back the photograph, slowly I nodded my head.

At length, with all the force of simplicity.

"Who was he?", I asked.

"Kit, my parent's youngest child. My brother, and Edward's, Christopher James Maitland."

Lady Aubrey fell silent for a moment, gazing out of the window, across the park, towards the low bell tower of the parish church, just visible above the trees.

"What happened?", I asked softly.

"It was his ninth birthday. My parents had rented a large house, up at

*Whistle . . .*

Whitcliffe, on the outskirts of Ludlow. That is, whilst certain repairs were put in hand here.

That afternoon Edward had promised to take Kit riding, out beyond Whitcliffe. As it was, luncheon came and went, by two o'clock there was still no sign of Edward. Kit became tired of waiting, and had one of the men in the stable yard saddle up his pony. Then he rode off on his own and that was the last anyone saw of him.

Edward arrived home about four and I remember he was feeling very pleased with himself. Earlier that morning he'd gone with friends to the races at Ludlow, and in the last race before luncheon, he'd been lucky enough to back a winner. Afterwards he and his friends had celebrated his good fortune with several drinks in the Member's Enclosure. In the excitement of the occasion, he'd completely forgotten his promise to take Kit riding. When I reminded him, he went straight down to the stable yard in search of his brother, only to be told the boy had ridden off on his own more than an hour previously.

To begin with no-one was unduly worried, but when it began to grow dark, and there was still no sign of Kit, my parents were informed. My father and brother organised the men from the estate, and a search of the surrounding countryside took place. It was hopeless of course, even though Kit couldn't have ridden very far, no-one knew which way he had gone. At dusk his pony was found wandering by itself, up on Whitcliffe Common, but of Kit, there was no trace, none whatsoever.

My mother took Kit's disappearance very badly and she never really got over it. The worst of it, I suppose, was not knowing what had happened.

My father on the other hand, blamed Edward, in fact he never forgave him. That apart, they never got on, right from when Edward was a little boy. My father seemed to find fault with everything he did but with Kit it was different as my parents, especially my father, idolised him. In a way I suppose Edward was partly to blame. He was always making rash promises, which he often failed to keep. After all, if he had..."

"Things might have turned out differently?"

"Exactly so, Mr Harris."

"And then?"

"After Kit vanished, relations between my father and brother became increasingly difficult. My mother was ill for much of the time. Of course by then Sir George and I were married, and living out in India, and then my mother died. Shortly after that Edward told my father about Mathilde, and that he planned on marrying her. That was the final straw. There was a terrible row and my father

*. . . and I'll be there*

ordered Edward off the estate. They never saw each other again. Perhaps if my father had but met her..."

She fell silent.

"And when the chance came for him to do so, it was too late. Shortly before her letter arrived here, my father suffered a massive stroke. It left him paralysed, without the power of speech or movement."

"And Frewen?"

"He was my father's under-keeper, up at Marsh Leys Hall. The house belonged to my grandmother and under the terms of her Will it was to pass, eventually, to Kit. She continued to live there, for several years, after her husband died. Before he went away to school in Hereford, Kit often stayed with her. She died a few months before he disappeared and after her death, the house was shut up.

When Kit vanished that part of the estate was never searched, for after all there was no need. Frewen told Edward he'd been out all day laying traps up in Marsh Leys Wood. If Kit had ridden up that way, he would have been bound to have seen him".

"And your brother believed him?"

"He had no real reason not to."

"No *real* reason?"

"Edward was certain he'd seen Frewen, with another man, coming out of a beer tent at the Ludlow races, but when my brother challenged Frewen as to his whereabouts that day, he protested his innocence, said Edward must be mistaken. And then, when Frewen's sister confirmed her brother's story..."

"Mrs Mcghie, your housekeeper?"

"Exactly so, and the day Kit vanished she was nursing her mother, up at the lodge. According to her, her brother never left Marsh Leys at all that day, not once. If Kit had ridden up that way, one of them would have been bound to have seen him and neither of them had."

"I see, but eventually Frewen left your father's service?"

"After his accident, yes, until then he remained as under-keeper, up at Marsh Leys."

"Accident?"

"Some months after Kit disappeared, my parents came out on an extended visit to India, to stay with my husband and myself. Father felt a complete change of scene might improve my mother's health and Edward was left in charge of the estate. While my parents were away, Frewen was thrown from his horse and badly injured."

*Whistle . . .*

"Where was this?", I asked.

"As it happens Mr Harris, up in Marsh Leys Wood, oddly enough Frewen always maintained something startled the animal. The fall left him with a permanent limp and obviously he couldn't continue as under-keeper, so my brother had no alternative but to discharge him. But Edward let Frewen's mother stay on at the lodge, even after he found another situation. After all it wasn't needed, not with the house being shut up."

"But that still doesn't explain why Frewen hated your brother so much. An eye for an eye was what he said, but when I asked him what he meant, he couldn't, or wouldn't, say."

"According to what his sister told me, her brother held Edward responsible for his son's death ... during the War."

"Jack Frewen?"

"Yes. When he was killed he was just sixteen years old, only four years older than Edward's own son. Jack Frewen should never have been in the army, let alone in France for he lied about his date of birth, in order to enlist."

"But what had that to do with your brother?"

"To begin with, nothing. You see when young Frewen first enlisted, he served in the Light Infantry's Seventh Battalion. As you may know Mr Harris, they suffered appalling casualties near Ypres and some of the survivors, including Jack Frewen, were transferred to the Fourth, my brother's Battalion."

"Your brother found out ...?"

"Eventually he did, and knowing the boy's true age, Edward made arrangements to have him sent home immediately."

"But that didn't happen?"

"No. The lad managed to talk Edward out of it. His aunt told me the boy wanted to "do his bit", like his elder brother, before the War was over. So Edward let him stay on in France - but as his orderly. That way the boy would at least be kept out of the trenches."

"Which was how he met your nephew."

"*Met him?* Christopher?"

"Yes, in Hereford. During the last Christmas of the War. Your brother brought young Frewen back with him, from France. Apparently Christopher took quite a shine to the lad and, in fact, I believe the feeling was mutual."

"I see."

"But even if your brother should have insisted on the boy being sent home, surely he cannot be held responsible for the lad's death?"

*... and I'll be there*

Lady Aubrey smiled, then sadly shook her head.

"But in a way you see he was, Mr Harris. The War was almost over and the fighting had all but died down. Everyone knew it was only a matter of time, perhaps only days, before the Armistice would be signed and they could all go home. Edward agreed to take Jack Frewen out with him, on what was to be their last patrol. On their way back to the British trenches, the lad saw a German helmet lying in the mud near a shell hole. Edward remarked it would make a fine souvenir for Christopher so Jack Frewen offered to go back and fetch it. Edward let him go but he shouldn't have of course. Young Frewen was shot trying to retrieve it and then the Germans began shelling the trench where Edward and the rest of his men had taken cover. In a matter of minutes they were cut to pieces and Harry Davies was the only survivor."

"Harry Davies?"

"He worked here on the estate, as a wheelwright, before the War. A stretcher party found him the next day. He'd been knocked unconscious, by the same shellburst which killed my brother. Davies spent several weeks in a military hospital near Arras. Then after the Armistice he was shipped back to England, to convalesce in Hereford. He came back here to his parent's cottage on the estate. Davies told me... what had happened to Edward."

"But in the meantime Frewen had found out from Davies ... how his son had died?"

Almost imperceptibly, Lady Aubrey nodded.

"Before I returned to England, Frewen visited Davies several times in hospital in Hereford and learnt how his son died. On the last occasion, just before Davies was discharged, Frewen made it perfectly clear he held my brother entirely responsible for the boy's death. In fact, he believed that Edward deliberately let his son be killed, because of what happened to Kit."

"Kit?"

"An eye for an eye. That was what Frewen told you, was it not?"

"Yes, but I fail to see what ..."

"Nor did I, until yesterday."

"Yesterday?"

"When I confronted Frewen's sister ... about other matters, she confirmed what Davies had told me. More importantly, told me the real reason why her brother blamed Edward for what had happened to his son."

I caught my breath.

"The real reason ..." I began, then stopped in mid-sentence.

99

*Whistle . . .*

"Do you remember my telling you of my brother's suspicions over Frewen's whereabouts on the day Kit vanished?"

"Your brother thought he'd seen Frewen at the races at Ludlow, but what of it?"

"As it turns out Edward was right, Frewen had indeed gone to the races that day. In fact, he spent the whole day there ... with his brother-in-law Daniel Mcghie."

"But then ... if Frewen wasn't up at Marsh Leys ... he couldn't have known whether Kit had ridden up there or not."

Lady Aubrey nodded.

"Precisely, but his sister did. I told you she was staying at the lodge, looking after her mother?"

"Yes..."

"Well, that afternoon, she saw Kit ride past on his way up the drive. That was the last she, or indeed anyone else, saw of him."

"So when Frewen lied about where he'd been ... said he hadn't seen the boy, the only way his sister could possibly support his story, was if she also denied having seen Kit?"

"Indeed."

"Presumably she had no idea where Kit went, after he rode past?"

"She says not, but where else would he be going, except up to the Hall? After all, the drive led nowhere else."

"Then somehow he found his way into the house and down into that cellar ..."

"You mentioned a broken grating, in the cellar wall."

I nodded.

"Several months after Kit vanished, Frewen was undertaking some minor repairs up at the Hall - my parents were thinking of letting the place - when he noticed a scrap of white cloth caught on the edge of the grating. I suppose Kit must have torn his shirt when he wriggled through. Suspecting intruders, Frewen made a search - he had a set of keys to the house down at the lodge - and found the remains of a young boy lying at the bottom of the well."

"Didn't he recognise who the boy was?"

Lady Aubrey paused, then swallowed.

"I understand the body was badly decomposed," she said softly.

"In any event, Frewen told no-one of what he had found?"

"Apart from his sister, no-one at all. It was her idea to collapse the sides of the shaft ... so as to hide better what it contained."

*. . . and I'll be there*

"An evil woman," I said dryly.

"And a commensurate liar," said Lady Aubrey coldly.

"That too."

"Dr Adams tells me in all likelihood the fall alone would have been enough to kill my brother. Death would have been instantaneous," Lady Aubrey paused.

"But you have your doubts?"

She nodded.

"I cannot but think if Frewen hadn't lied ... if his sister hadn't told the same tale, Kit might yet have been found alive. If only Edward had ordered a search to be made up at Marsh Leys ..."

"Then, when stories began to circulate ... about a young boy ... being seen near the house ... did no-one seek to investigate?"

"By then it was too late, my husband and I were already in India. My mother had died and Edward and my father had quarrelled. Apart from that, my father would never have believed them, for after all, who would have credited them to be true? Idle gossip in the servant's quarters, round the estate, in the town, nothing more."

"And ... the remains, found in the well ... after the fire? There can be no doubt, no doubt of any kind? Kit?"

"None at all as this was found with them, at the bottom of the shaft. My brother must have had it in his pocket, when he fell ..."

She was holding something in the palm of her outstretched hand. Something small. Something wooden.

"Take it Mr Harris, please."

I reached forward and took it from her. It was a little wooden whistle, choked with dirt. I turned it round in my hands. Carved in the wood were the letters C.J.M ... Christopher James Maitland.

"I should like you to have it Mr Harris, as a keepsake."

"But, Lady Aubrey, it was your brother's. Rightly it belongs to ..."

"No, I insist."

"Then, thankyou, I shall treasure it." My voice was strangely uneven, almost husky.

"On that last morning, Edward had given it to Kit, as a birthday present, here, in this very room." Her voice sank almost to a whisper, almost as if she were shying away from phantoms. "I even remember what Edward said. We laughed about it at the time."

Lady Aubrey paused as I sat and waited while she regained her composure.

*Whistle . . .*

That done, she raised her head and her eyes were now free from tears, but as she spoke her voice was trembling.

"Well, Kit, if you ever get yourself into a scrape, all you have to do is whistle. **Whistle and I'll be there**."

Lady Aubrey paused, then she continued.

"Earlier this afternoon Mr Harris, I told you my brother Edward was very good at making promises which he then failed to honour. But this time someone was there to take his place ... to answer Kit's call for help." She paused and looked directly at me, "you, Mr Harris."

In the ensuing silence, she reached across and clasped my hand. Her blue eyes, dark with memories long suppressed, held mine. Outside the window the blackbird had ceased to sing.

# Whistle and I'll be There

Later that same month I returned to Evans, Chapman and Jenkins, but although I attempted to immerse myself in my work, it soon became clear that a complete change of scene was imperative, were I ever to be able to throw off the shadows of the past.

Through the good offices of Mr Chapman, I became aware of a situation which had arisen at Broome, Challoner and Deakin here in Norwich. Although the post did not command quite as high a salary as I had enjoyed in Hereford, it was nevertheless more than acceptable. I was fortunate enough to be offered the position, which I accepted with alacrity.

Shortly before I left to take up my new duties in Norwich, Claire and I were married in All Saints' Church, Hereford. It was a modest affair as weddings go for, like Claire, I had been an only child, and neither of us wanted a great deal of fuss. Mathilde Montcontour and Christopher both came to the ceremony. Along with her good wishes for the future, Lady Aubrey sent us a handsome dinner service as a wedding gift.

So the years passed and I never left Broome, Challoner and Deakin, remaining with them until I retired, by which time I had achieved the position of Senior Partner. Simon and Andrew were born and in due course went their respective ways. Mathilde Montcontour and I corresponded regularly for many years, she never married, choosing instead to remain faithful to Edward's memory. Not long after Christopher attained his majority, she returned to Canada, her uncle Henri having died and left her his property in Quebec. Andrew stayed with her for a brief time following his acceptance of the lectureship offered to him by Mcgill University, before, with her help, finding suitable lodgings in Montreal.

Claire and I were happy and content, and even if we were no longer young, both of us were in good health, facing the prospect of old age with equanimity. I assumed what was past was over, finished and done with. Naïve of me perhaps, but after all I had no reason to think otherwise. Not until yesterday, and the birthday of our youngest grandson, David.

I should have realised, of course, that happiness is not a possession. It is far too ephemeral for that, dependant as it is upon one's state of mind. Indeed, over the last few days, my sense of foreboding, of impending disaster, had increased, made worse by the gnawing fear that it lay within my power to avert the coming calamity, if only

*Whistle...*

I could discover what it was. Yet, other than the recurrence of my old nightmare, there really was nothing to account for it. I put some of my *malaise* down to the appalling weather, which had been unseasonably wet for the time of the year, the Wensum running dangerously high all the way southwards from Fakenham.

Saturday was a day of blustery, squally showers. That morning, Claire and myself, accompanied by both Tim and young David, were all driven down to Thorpe station, here in Norwich. The two boys wrestled like puppies on the back seat of the Bentley nearly all the way there, ignoring Claire's admonishments to stop, only finally desisting when I sharply told them enough was enough, and unless they behaved themselves, I would have Armstrong stop the motor, and they would have to get out and walk the rest of the way to the station on foot.

It was, I reflected somewhat ruefully, just as well that Tim had been asked to spend the week-end with a school friend in Wymondham, particularly when, much to David's *chagrin*, Tim had deliberately chosen, that very morning at the breakfast table, to announce to the assembled company that at the advanced age of twelve, *he* was much to old for parties. David retorted that he hadn't been invited anyway, whereupon Tim, in a telling display of his new found maturity, proceeded to pelt his younger brother with bread pellets, whenever he thought he could do so without being observed.

Much to Tim's embarrassment, Claire was travelling with him as far as Wymondham, and then on to North Elmham, to visit an elderly maiden aunt. Claire was not expected back much before midnight that same day, while Tim would not be returning until after tea on Sunday evening.

So, after having seen them both off from the station, David and I had the rest of the day to ourselves. Having returned to the house, we spent the remainder of the morning seated in front of the study fire, pasting stamps into one of my leather bound albums, while outside the rain spattered against the window panes.

After luncheon the weather improved somewhat. So, leaving David in the capable hands of Mrs Holt, I had Armstrong drive me over to the coast for a breath of sea air. I took the dogs with me as I felt the exercise would do them good too. Armstrong stopped the motor at a spot just north of Happisburgh where there was easy access down onto the beach, not far from Walcott as it happened. Of course, the very name should have served as a warning, but I never gave it a moment's thought.

Not surprisingly, I had the beach to myself, and spent a pleasant, if bracing, afternoon walking along the sea strand, the two dogs gambolling along behind me at my heels, or chasing the pebbles I skimmed for them into the water.

*. . . and I'll be there*

By the time I came to retrace my steps, dusk was fast falling, also, judging by the white water out on the shoals, there was every prospect of a very stormy night ahead.

It was as I made my way back along the desolate shoreline, that I had the oddest impression that someone was dogging my footsteps, though how I knew that I could not say. Not that I was unduly worried, after all, I had Jiggs and Rufus with me, and I was already in sight of the motor car. In fact, I could even make out the hunched figure of Armstrong sitting in the driver's seat, pouring over his crossword.

A few moments later, and I was crunching through the loose shingle, up onto the road, the dogs scrambling on behind. Just then I chanced to look back and noticed that the light was fading rapidly now, but by the seaward end of one of the wooden groynes, which bisected the beach at regular intervals, I saw a young lad, standing motionless by the edge of the water. He seemed to be looking directly at me and I was surprised that I hadn't noticed him before. Presumably he must have been sheltering in the lee of one of the groynes, otherwise I could not have failed to see him.

Oddly enough, there seemed to be something vaguely familiar about him, particularly the way he stood, although at that distance and in poor light, it was impossible to be sure. In any event, the likelihood that we knew each other was extremely remote. After all, I was not given to numbering beachcombers among my acquaintances, professional or otherwise - although in my time I had represented several colourful characters in court.

Suddenly, and for no apparent reason, I found myself shivering.

"Help me, please," said a voice very distinctly in my ear. I whirled round and at the same time a gull passing close overhead gave a loud, derisive squawk.

"I was asking if you needed any help with the dogs, sir," said Armstrong, opening the rear door of the motor car.

"No, I can manage, thankyou," I said stiffly.

I climbed thankfully inside the car, just as the first few drops of rain began to fall. A moment or two later, with the rain drumming on the roof, myself ensconced on the back seat, the two dogs panting at my feet, we set off back towards Norwich.

By the time I reached Blakeney Lodge, it was already quite dark. During the journey back, the wind had risen to near gale force, the rain driving against the windows of the Bentley with ever increasing ferocity. Bidding the chauffeur goodnight, I got out of the car at the front door, the dogs padding behind me, leaving Armstrong to drive the motor round to its garage in the old stableblock.

*Whistle . . .*

Inside the hall the lamps were lit, radiating light and warmth into the rainswept darkness. I glanced at the barometer by the front door. It had fallen so low that I wondered if it was still reliable. I hoped it was not.

Having already had his tea served him in the servants' kitchen by Mrs Holt, freshly washed and scrubbed, in striped pyjamas and dressing gown, David was waiting up for me in the hall to say goodnight. He hugged and kissed me, then ran off upstairs to bed. As I watched him scamper up the main staircase I wondered if he would get much sleep. The noise of the storm apart, he was far too excited about what the morrow would bring.

After a light supper, served to me in the library, I reached down a volume at random from off the shelves and sat by the fire, the dogs stretched out on the hearthrug in front of me. I opened the book I had selected at the title page. By sheer chance, the volume I had chosen was George Borrow's *Wild Wales*.

Despite the curtains being drawn and the shutters closed, both dogs seemed unusually distressed by the noise of the storm. So much so, that several times during the next hour, each of them in turn sniffed the air, got up and ran over to the windows overlooking the terrace, where, despite my attempts to silence them, they continued to yelp furiously for several minutes at a time.

In the end I gave up trying to read. Having called James in to take both the dogs downstairs, I wished him goodnight, and, taking my book with me, retired upstairs.

Having washed, I undressed and climbed into bed, where I made a desultory attempt at trying to resume reading, but the sound of the wind made it difficult to concentrate and, once again, I gave up. Instead I lay awake listening to the noise of the storm for some time; the rain driving against the casements, the wind howling round the outside of the house, wailing like a banshee, in fact I could almost imagine I felt the house swaying to and fro. Come morning I wondered if we would have lost any more trees.

After a while I must have fallen asleep, because the next thing I recall was suddenly waking up. At least I think I woke up, although I was probably somewhere on that borderline which exists between sleep and consciousness. The book I had been reading was lying face down on the floor by the side of the bed, so I naturally assumed it must have been the sound of it hitting the floorboards which had awoken me.

Soft footfalls sounded in the passage outside my room. I thought it must be David, frightened by the storm, but then, as I thought about it, I remembered the night nursery lay across the landing in the other wing of the house. If David was frightened by the noise of the storm, he was far more likely to ring for Janet

*. . . and I'll be there*

or one of the other servants, rather than leave the warmth and safety of his bed and try to find his way across to this side of the house in the darkness all on his own.

I glanced over at the other side of the bed. It had not been slept in, so evidently Claire had not yet returned. I looked at my watch, it was just after midnight.

"Claire?" I called out sleepily, "Is that you?" There was not reply so I suppose I must have fallen asleep again shortly afterwards, if in fact I'd ever been awake in the first place.

The following morning I was awoken by the sound of the heavy curtains being drawn back, sunlight flooded into the bedroom.

"Good morning, sir."

James laid the breakfast tray and a folded newspaper on the empty side of the bed.

"Good morning," I replied, struggling to sit up. "Is Mrs Harris not yet returned?" I asked a little anxiously.

"I understand that she returned a little later than anticipated sir. I had Ethel make a bed up for her in Master Andrew's old room, so as not to disturb you. I trust that was in order, sir."

"Yes, perfectly in order, thankyou, James," I said, somewhat distractedly.

After breakfast, I washed, shaved and dressed, then went downstairs. The house was a hive of activity. In fact, the preparations for David's birthday party had already occupied both Claire and Mrs Holt for the better part of a week. I must concede that a rambling great house such as this, with its outbuildings and extensive grounds, lends itself to such an occasion like no other. Young David was running about the place, driving everyone to distraction. Wishing him a very 'Happy Birthday', wisely I retreated to the comparative tranquillity of my study to read my paper.

By the time I joined Claire in the morning room for an early coffee, the weather had changed and it had begun to rain heavily once again. That morning we were both attending the annual Service of Remembrance in the cathedral, something we have done each Armistice Day since our arrival in Norwich. Because of the inclement weather, we half expected to have to call for Armstrong to bring the motor car round to the front door, but then, just before we were due to leave for the Service, the rain stopped and the sun came out.

Leaving Mrs Holt in sole charge of the final preparations for the afternoon's festivities, and telling David to keep out from under everyone's feet, Claire and I set off on foot, bound for the cathedral.

*Whistle . . .*

Just after one o'clock we returned to the house, to find the hall a blaze of colour. Balloons and Chinese lanterns hung from the plaster ceiling, while brightly coloured paper streamers festooned the dark panelling.

Flanked on either side by two benches dragged in from the servants' kitchen, a long trestle table ran down the entire length of the room. It was covered by a snowy white linen cloth, which in turn was decked with glasses and plates, jugs of lemonade, piles of sandwiches, sausages on sticks, shortbread and biscuits. In the centre of the table, resplendent in its isolation, was an enormous birthday cake. From somewhere deep within the recesses of her storecupboards, Mrs Holt had even managed to rustle up several unopened boxes of crackers left over from the previous Christmas.

In the midst of all the ordered chaos, dressed in the army uniform Claire had made him specially for the occasion, David was running about, whooping like some demented dervish.

Smiling to ourselves, we escaped into the dining room, where we enjoyed a light luncheon, after which Claire retired upstairs to rest, while I went into my study to write some letters.

The calm before the storm.

From two o'clock onwards, albeit temporarily, peace and tranquillity fled the house, as a succession of excited young boys from David's school, all in fancy dress, began arriving at Blakeney Lodge, each clutching a present, neatly purloined by David as soon as they stepped through the front door. Some of their parents, who had kindly agreed to help Claire and I oversee the festivities, had also entered into the spirit of the occasion and had dressed up in a variety of costumes.

Nothing untoward occurred until about four o'clock that afternoon, when Claire asked me to call the boys in for tea.

As I stepped out onto the upper terrace, I was assailed by a veritable barrage of shouting and yelling. Somewhere, down amongst the rhododendrons, a mock battle was being waged, no doubt initiated by David for whom weapons and warfare have always held a peculiar fascination. The conflict raging as far as the banks of the Wensum at the bottom of the garden, "So much for the Armistice," I thought.

I strolled leisurely down across the gardens, as far as the lower terrace. Resting my hands on the stone balustrade, I leaned over and called to the youthful combatants that tea was ready. The noise of battle ceased almost immediately, evidently the troops were hungry. Smiling to myself, thrusting my hands deep into

*. . . and I'll be there*

my pockets, I turned away, and began to walk slowly back towards the house.

Scarcely had I taken more than half a dozen steps, when suddenly I froze in my tracks. I stood still and listened intently. Because for me, the silence which followed the temporary cessation of hostilities, had been shattered, by the sound of a penny whistle ... the whistle which lay locked away in the bottom drawer of my desk, as it had been for nearly half a century.

Shouting with laughter, their mock battle postponed until after tea, the boys came running, across the lawns, up the steps, and along the terrace.

All that was, except David.

I called out to one of them, a fair haired young lad with a freckled face, dressed as a pirate with a black patch over his left eye.

"Where's David?"

"Oh, he'll be along in a minute, sir, he's just talking to someone ... down there, by the boat-house". The boy pointed towards the lower part of the garden.

*"Who?"*

"A man sir, I don't know his name. *He's* dressed up too sir," he added excitedly.

"As what?" I asked. Somehow I knew what the boy's answer would be before he answered me.

"Why sir, like David, as a soldier. Are *you* alright, sir?"

I didn't stop to answer. Instead, I turned and began to run, as fast as I have ever run, across the lawn, down through the shrubbery, towards the boat-house and the river at the bottom of the garden.

Several minutes later I emerged scratched and breathless onto the narrow patch of short grass between the rain-soaked rhododendrons and the river bank. As I did so, the uniformed figure of a man slowly emerged from the shadows of the boat-house and I felt my blood run cold. I found myself rooted to the spot, paralysed by fear, for there was no mistaking who it was.

Frewen.

He looked directly at me, a mocking, malignant smile played about the corners of his mouth. Slowly he raised his arm and pointed towards the river. Seemingly powerless to do anything other than as I was bidden, I found myself looking in the same direction. It was then that I saw David.

Alongside the boat-house, and once used by Simon and Andrew to practice their diving, a narrow dilapidated wooden jetty, ran out for some distance above the surface of the water. David was right at the far end of the jetty, kneeling down, apparently intent on staring at something in the water, while less than two feet below him the river foamed and surged round the wooden piers.

*Whistle...*

To my horror, fifty yards upstream of where David was kneeling, swept along by the fast flowing waters of the river, a tangled mass of driftwood was moving swiftly towards the end of the jetty. David seemed not to have seen it, in fact he appeared completely oblivious to where he was.

I tried to cry out, to warn David of the danger he was in, but found I could neither move nor speak. All I could do was stand and watch, a helpless spectator to the unfolding tragedy.

Then suddenly, above the noise of the flood water:-

"Help me, please," a small voice said insistently in my ear. The voice was David's, although that was clearly impossible, but it was enough. Those three words were all it took to give me back my power of speech and movement. I raced across the short stretch of turf which was all that separated me from the landward end of the jetty, yelling myself hoarse above the roar of the water.

"David, for God's sake, get off there," I screamed.

The mass of driftwood was less than twenty yards away now, bearing down on the end of the jetty with the speed and inexorable purpose of an express train. For one awful moment I thought David hadn't heard me. Then suddenly he turned his head and saw the danger.

"David!"

"Grandfather!"

"Run David, run," whereupon he turned and began to run, pounding down the length of the rickety jetty, back towards dry land and safety, the wooden boards bouncing under his feet. He was no more than half way along, when, with a sickening crunch, the mass of driftwood smashed into the end of the jetty. The whole structure shook and the boards tilted.

David all but lost his footing. Somehow he managed to check himself and regained his balance. A moment or two later and he had reached the river bank. As he did so, there came the awful sound of wood splintering, and the end of the jetty collapsed into the surging waters, and was swept away on the flood tide. Of Frewen there was no trace, none whatsoever.

Shaken by his narrow escape, somewhat unsteadily, David walked towards me across the grass.

"Are you alright?"

"I ... think so." David was looking anxiously about him.

"Where's he gone?" he asked nervously.

"Where's who gone?"

"The soldier, he was standing right next to me ... on the end of the jetty. Didn't you see him grandfather? He was telling me all about the War and about his son, Jack, he ... "

"No ... I didn't," I lied, "I was more concerned about you." I was shaking, and my breath was coming in rapid painful gasps. Heedless of the wet grass I knelt down, and placed both my hands firmly on David's young shoulders.

"How many times have I told you about that old jetty? You can't even swim." David looked crestfallen.

"I'm sorry," he mumbled.

"Well," I said, breathing a deep sigh of relief and running my fingers through his hair, "no harm done. Time we were getting back, otherwise there won't be any tea left. Come on."

I set off back towards the house and David fell in beside me. At the top of the first flight of steps, some sixth sense made me stop and turn round. A chill ran down the length of my spine, the chill of the secret cold.

This time, of course, I recognised him at once. The boy was standing some distance away, at the far end of what remained of the jetty. For one brief instant our eyes met, then slowly he raised his hand, something he'd never done before. Instinctively I did the same, for the debt he owed me had been paid.

"Who are you waving to grandfather?" David tugged impatiently at my sleeve.

"Sorry David, what did you say?" I looked down at his earnest little face beneath its mop of tousled black hair.

"Who were you waving to?" he repeated.

"Oh, just someone I once knew," David looked thoughtfully at me for a moment, while my heart skipped a beat. After all, what else could I say? Then slowly he nodded his head. Thankfully, my answer seemed to satisfy him and I breathed a silent heartfelt sigh of relief.

"Race you to the house, grandfather."

"I'll give you a head start, and mind you don't fall." David grinned back at me, then without further ado ran off across the wet lawns towards the house.

I turned and looked back at the jetty, but the boy had already disappeared. I knew then that I would never see him again.